What Makes a Father

Teresa Southwick

P9-CQQ-423

HARLEQUIN® SPECIAL EDITION

If you purchased this book without a cover you should be aware that this book is stolen property. It was reported as "unsold and destroyed" to the publisher, and neither the author nor the publisher has received any payment for this "stripped book."

Recycling programs
for this product may
not exist in your area.

ISBN-13: 978-1-335-57415-2

What Makes a Father

Copyright © 2019 by Teresa Southwick

All rights reserved. Except for use in any review, the reproduction or utilization of this work in whole or in part in any form by any electronic, mechanical or other means, now known or hereafter invented, including xerography, photocopying and recording, or in any information storage or retrieval system, is forbidden without the written permission of the publisher, Harlequin Enterprises Limited, 22 Adelaide St. West, 40th Floor, Toronto, Ontario M5H 4E3, Canada.

This is a work of fiction. Names, characters, places and incidents are either the product of the author's imagination or are used fictitiously, and any resemblance to actual persons, living or dead, business establishments, events or locales is entirely coincidental.

This edition published by arrangement with Harlequin Books S.A.

For questions and comments about the quality of this book, please contact us at CustomerService@Harlequin.com.

® and TM are trademarks of Harlequin Enterprises Limited or its corporate affiliates. Trademarks indicated with ® are registered in the United States Patent and Trademark Office, the Canadian Intellectual Property Office and in other countries.

Printed in U.S.A.

"I suppose that means you don't want to sign away your rights as a father."

"No." Mason's expression was intense, serious. "In fact, since I last saw you, I consulted an attorney."

Words to put fear into a girl's heart. "I'm their legal guardian. If you try to take them away from me—"

"Whoa." He put his hands up in a "slow down" motion. "It's just that even though I'm their father, I have no rights because my name isn't on the birth certificates. Now, with DNA proof, I will acknowledge paternity and petition the court to legally claim my paternal rights."

"How long will that take?"

"There's a sixty-day waiting period, then however long it takes to get a court date," he said.

"And then you're going to sue for sole custody?"

"Of course not. No one is talking custody fight here. You clearly love them, Annie."

"I do. But how can you know that?" Where men were concerned, suspicion was her default emotion.

"Because you did copious research on a pacifier. And I just get the feeling if I look at either baby funny, you'd cut my heart out with a spoon."

"You're not wrong." But how did he know her so well? They'd barely met.

Dear Reader,

I can't imagine having twins, the challenges involved in taking care of two babies at the same time. One was hard enough for me!

In *What Makes a Father*, Annie Campbell unexpectedly becomes the legal guardian of newborn twins when her beloved sister passes away from complications of childbirth. On top of that, Annie doesn't know who the father is. Her sister narrowed the possibilities down to three. As much as she would prefer to raise her niece and nephew without fatherly interference, especially from a complete stranger, she feels a moral obligation to notify the mystery man.

Army emergency specialist Dr. Mason Blackburne is deployed when he receives a message that he might be the father of twins. A family is something he's always wanted, and when he returns home, the first place he goes is to meet the babies. And the surprises keep on coming when he gets to know the woman caring for them. Their aunt is protective, stubborn, exhausted and way more intriguing than this romantically disillusioned doctor would like.

Annie and Mason meet under extraordinary circumstances and bond over their love for two babies. They share the goal of giving them a traditional family and end up falling in love against their better judgment. I hope this story touches your heart as much as it did mine.

Enjoy!

Teresa Southwick

Teresa Southwick lives with her husband in Las Vegas, the city that reinvents itself every day. An avid fan of romance novels, she is delighted to be living out her dream of writing for Harlequin.

Books by Teresa Southwick

Harlequin Special Edition

The Bachelors of Blackwater Lake

Finding Family...and Forever?
One Night with the Boss
The Rancher Who Took Her In
A Decent Proposal
The Widow's Bachelor Bargain
How to Land Her Lawman
A Word with the Bachelor
Just a Little Bit Married
The New Guy in Town
His by Christmas
Just What the Cowboy Needed
What Makes a Father

Montana Mavericks: The Lonelyhearts Ranch

Unmasking the Maverick

Montana Mavericks: The Baby Bonanza

Her Maverick M.D.

**Montana Mavericks:
What Happened at the Wedding?**

An Officer and a Maverick

Montana Mavericks: 20 Years in the Saddle!

From Maverick to Daddy

Visit the Author Profile page at Harlequin.com for more titles.

To my parents, Gladys and Frank Boyle.
You made raising six kids look easy.
I love you both and miss you always.

Chapter One

Annie Campbell didn't know exhaustion of this magnitude was even possible. Since suddenly becoming a mom to newborn twins three months ago, she'd been tired, but in the last week she'd counted sleep in seconds and minutes rather than hours. Either Charlie or Sarah was always awake, hungry, wet, crabby or crying uncontrollably for no apparent reason. Childhood had been challenging for Annie, but raising twins was the hardest thing she'd ever done.

And she wouldn't trade being their mom for anything. With one toothless grin they had her wrapped around their little fingers. Now they had all the symptoms of teething—drooling, gnawing on their fists, crying—and Annie honestly wasn't sure she'd survive it.

Her apartment was small, perfect for a single woman. Then she brought infants home from the hospital, forced by circumstances to care for two babies at once and too overwhelmed to look for a bigger place. And she was still overwhelmed. On a good day she could sneak in a shower. Today hadn't been a good day but there were hopeful signs.

Sarah was quiet in the crib. Charlie was in her arms but she could feel him relaxing, possibly into sleep. Oh, please God. She would walk until her legs fell off if that's what it took. With luck he'd go quietly in with his sister and Annie could close her eyes. To heck with a shower.

Slowly she did a circuit of the living room, past the bar that separated it from the kitchen, around the oak coffee table, gliding by the window that looked out on the center courtyard of the apartment complex. As the baby grew heavier in her arms, she could almost feel victory in her grasp, the euphoria of having two babies asleep at the same time.

Then some fool rang her doorbell. Charlie jerked awake and started to cry just on general principle. Sarah's wails came from the bedroom.

"Someone is going to pay." Annie cuddled the startled baby closer and kissed his head. "Not you, Charlie bear. You're perfect. But if someone is selling something they'll get more than they bargained for."

She peeked through the front window and saw a man wearing military camouflage. This was probably daddy candidate number three, the last one on her sister's list of men who might be the babies' father. This had to be Mason Blackburne, the army doctor who'd been deployed to Afghanistan. She'd contacted him by email and he'd claimed he'd get back to her right away when he returned to the States. She hadn't expected that he actually would.

In her experience, men were selfish, hurtful and unreliable. His written response was a brush-off any idiot would see. Except maybe not since he was standing outside. Not to be picky, but the least he could have done was call first. Come to think of it, how did he get her address? She'd only given him her phone number in the email. Apparently she was taking too long because he followed up the doorbell ring with an aggressive knock.

The chain locking the door was in place so she opened it just a crack. "Your timing sucks."

"Annie Campbell? I'm Mason Blackburne."

"I gave you my number. You were supposed to call me. How did you get my address?"

"From Jessica."

Pain sliced through Annie when she heard her sister's name. Jess had died shortly after giving birth to the twins. The joy of welcoming her niece and nephew into the world turned to unimaginable grief at losing the person Annie loved most in the world. Her sister had lived with her off and on, couch surfing when she needed somewhere to stay. She didn't trust men in general any more than Annie, so if she'd given the address to this guy, her gut must have said he was okay.

Annie unlocked the door and opened it. For the first time she got a good look at Mason Blackburne. Two things stood out: he was tall, and his eyes were startlingly blue. And he was boyishly handsome. Okay, that was three things, but she was too tired to care. And some part of her worn-out brain was regretting that her hair was in a messy ponytail because she hadn't washed it. Or showered today. Or put on makeup. And she was wearing baggy sweatpants and an oversize T-shirt.

"Come in," she said, stepping back. "I've got a DNA swab right here. Just rub it on the inside of each cheek for thirty seconds and put it back in the tube. I'll send it to the lab with the other one and the results will be back in five business days."

But it wasn't clear whether or not he'd heard her. The guy was staring at Charlie. The baby had stopped crying and was staring suspiciously back at the tall stranger. And he was sucking his thumb. The baby, not the stranger.

She sighed. "Well, baby boy, now all my extensive research into the best pacifier on the planet to prevent thumb-sucking is down the tubes. Somewhere an orthodontist is doing the dance of joy."

Mason had a look of awe on his face. "What's his name?"

"Charlie."

"Did Jessica choose that?"

"No, she didn't get a chance. But she'd narrowed down the choices to Christopher and Charles. Sarah was always the top girls' name."

He looked past her to the hallway where the baby girl was still crying. "Can I see her?"

Annie wanted to say no. She didn't know this guy from a rock, but again, Jess didn't normally share her address with men and she'd given it to him. So maybe it was okay.

After closing the front door, she headed for the hallway with daddy candidate number three following. The master bedroom and bath were on the right, and across from it was her office, now the twins' nursery.

"She's in here. And before you ask, they share the crib. The pediatrician advised not separating them just yet."

"Because they shared quarters for nine months," he said.

"Exactly." They walked into the room where the crib was on the wall opposite her desk. "She probably needs her diaper changed. I'll have to put Charlie down since I haven't yet figured out how to do it one-handed. Fair warning—he's going to cry."

"Could I hold him?"

Annie's gaze snapped to his face. "Why?"

"You need help. And he might be my son." There was

an edge to his voice and intensity in his eyes that made her think it really mattered to him.

Annie thought it over. This guy *might* be Charlie's father. Why not push him into the deep end of the pool, let him know what he was getting into. She held Charlie out to him and he took the baby, a little awkwardly.

Annie walked over to the crib and lowered the side rail. She picked up the little girl to comfort her first. "It's okay, Sarah. You're fine. I'm here, sweet girl. I have to put you down again, just for a minute to change that diaper. Trust me on this. You'll feel a lot better."

Three months ago the top of her lateral file cabinet had become the storage area for diaper supplies. She settled the baby back in the crib and quickly swapped the wet diaper for a dry one, then picked her up again for a snuggle.

"What happened to Jessica?" He looked away from the baby and met her gaze.

"I told you in the email. She had a pulmonary embolism, a blood clot in her—"

"Lung. I'm a doctor. I get it. But why didn't she let me know she was pregnant? And that I might be the father of the baby—" He stopped and his gaze settled on Sarah. *"Babies?"*

"I told her more than once that the biological father had a right to know. Even though I suggested she let the guy screw up first, she was convinced that he would desert her anyway. She planned to raise them by herself."

"Why would she think that?" There was a tinge of exasperation and outrage in his tone.

"She had her reasons."

His gaze narrowed and irritation pushed out the baby awe. "So you talked her into it? She didn't intend to share the information."

"Not with you or the other two men she slept with."

Annie winced as those words came out of her mouth. That made Jess sound like a slut. Maybe it was a little bit true, but that's not who she was. Her sister liked men and sex. She'd been looking for fun, nothing more. "Men sleep around all the time and no one thinks less of them. But if a woman does it, she's trash. Don't you dare judge her."

"I wasn't judging—"

"Oh, please." When a person was as tired as she was, that person had to dig deep for patience. Hers was dangerously depleted. She looked at him and, judging by the uncertain expression on his face, it was possible that there were flames shooting out of her eyes. "And why is this all on my sister? You were a willing participant. Who didn't wear a condom."

"I just wanted to talk," he protested.

"Right. That's what they all say." Her voice dripped with sarcasm. "You should know that I'm not normally this abrasive, but I'm tired. And I was much more compassionate the first two times a potential father showed up—"

"What happened with them?"

"First one wasn't a match. Number two finally came by a few days ago. I have his sample for the lab along with a legal document from his attorney relinquishing all rights to the babies in exchange for my signed agreement not to pursue him for child support should he be a match. I was only too happy to do that and send him responsibility-free on his way. Sarah and Charlie deserve to be wanted more than anything. They don't need a person like that in their lives."

"Prince of a guy." Mason was still holding Charlie and lightly rubbed a big hand over the baby's back.

Annie loved her sister but that didn't mean she approved of her choices in men. "A few weeks before she gave birth, Jess had second thoughts and narrowed down potential daddy candidates to three. Before she could contact them, she went into labor and showed symptoms of the embolism. Tests confirmed it and the risks were explained to her. She got scared for the babies if something should happen to her and put in writing that I would be the guardian. It was witnessed by two nurses and is a legally binding agreement. No one really thought she would die, but fate didn't cooperate. Now Charlie and Sarah are my babies and I will do anything and everything to keep them safe."

"I'm a doctor. I took an oath to do no harm."

"There are a lot of ways to damage children besides physically." Annie knew from experience that emotional wounds could be every bit as painful and were the ones you didn't have to hide with makeup or a story about being clumsy. "And I wasn't implying that you would hurt them."

"I would never do that," he said fervently.

For the first time she noticed that he looked every bit as tired as she felt. And he was wearing a military uniform—if camouflage was considered a uniform. What was his deal? "When did you get back from Afghanistan?"

"A couple of hours ago. My family lives in Huntington Hills, but I haven't seen them yet."

"You came here first? From the airport?"

"Yes."

It was hard not to be impressed by that but somehow Annie managed. The adrenaline surge during her outburst had drained her reserves and she wanted to be done with this, and him. "Look, if you'd please just do the DNA swab and leave your contact information for the lab, that would be great. Five business days and we'll know."

"Okay." Gently, he put Charlie down in the crib.

Annie did the same with Sarah and miraculously the two didn't immediately start to cry. "Follow me."

They went to her small kitchen, where the sink was full of baby bottles and dishes waiting to be washed.

"I have the kits here." She grabbed one from the counter and handed it to him. He seemed to know what to do.

Mason took the swab out of the tube and expertly rubbed it on the inside of his cheek for the required amount of time, then packaged it up and filled out the paperwork. "That should do it."

"I'll send it to the lab along with the other one."

"Okay."

"Thank you. Not to be rude, but would you please go?"

He started to say something, then stopped and simply let himself out the front door without a word.

Annie breathed a sigh of relief. The uncertainty would be over in five business days but somehow that didn't ease her mind as much as she'd thought it would. After meeting Mason Blackburne, she wasn't sure whether or not she wanted to share child custody with him. Not because he would be difficult, but because he wouldn't. And that could potentially be worse.

"She researched pacifiers, Mom." Mason stopped pacing the kitchen long enough to look at the woman who'd given birth to him. "I don't know whether or not she's a good mother, but both babies were clean, well-fed and happy. Well, one or the other was crying, but it was normal crying, if you know what I mean."

"I do," Florence Blackburne said wryly. "And it's not like she staged the scene. She had no idea you were going to stop by."

"That's true." He'd arrived home five days ago and told her everything. He'd started his job as an ER doctor and he was house hunting. None of it took his mind off the fact that he might be a father.

"That poor woman. Losing her sister and now raising two infants by herself." His mom was shaking her head and there was sympathy in her eyes. "I don't know what I would have done without your father when you and your siblings were born. And I only had one baby at a time."

"Yeah. She looked really exhausted." Pretty in spite of that, he thought. He remembered Jessica and Annie looked a lot like her. But their personalities were very different. Jess was a little wild, living on the edge. Annie seemed maternal, nurturing. Protective. Honest. The kind of woman he'd want to raise his children. If they *were* his children.

The lab hadn't notified him yet, but this was business day number five and he kept looking at his phone to make sure he hadn't missed the call.

"Checking your cell isn't going to make the news come any faster. I'm sure the twins are yours." His mother gave him her "mom" look, full of understanding and support.

She loved kids and had four of them, never for a moment letting on that she'd sacrificed anything on their behalf. Mason was wired like her and badly wanted kids of his own. The woman he'd married had shared that dream, and the heartbreak of not being able to realize it had broken them up. The third miscarriage had cost him his child and his wife—he'd lost his whole family. If the experience had taught him anything, it was not to have expectations or get his hopes up.

"If only DNA results happened as fast in real life as they do on TV," he said.

"Did the babies look like you?" Flo asked. "Eye color? Shape of the face? That strong, square jaw," she teased.

"They actually looked a lot like Annie. Their aunt. Hazel eyes. Blond hair. Pretty." Something he didn't share with his mother was that Annie Campbell had a very nice ass. Her baggy sweats had hid that asset, no pun intended, until she'd bent over to pick up a toy on the floor. There was no doubt in his mind that a shower and good night's sleep would transform her into a woman who would turn heads on the street. "DNA is the only way to be sure."

"That's just science. It's no match for maternal instinct. And mine is telling me that those babies are my grand-children."

"Don't, Mom."

"What?" she asked innocently.

"If you have expectations, you're going to be let down." Mason could give a seminar on strategies to avoid disappointment. The only surefire approach was to turn off emotion. Not until the science said it was okay could you let yourself care.

Flo's face took on a familiar expression, the one that said she knew what he was thinking and wanted to take away his pain. The woman was a force of nature and if she couldn't do something, it couldn't be done. Wisely she stayed silent about his past and the situation that had left him bruised and battered. And bitter.

There was something to be said for Jessica's philosophy of fun without complications. But Annie was right, too. He hadn't used a condom and chose to believe the woman who'd said she had everything taken care of. Now he was on pins and needles waiting for the results of a test that could potentially change his life forever.

It was almost five o'clock and the lab's business hours were nearly over for the day. Maybe Annie hadn't sent the samples as soon as she'd planned to. She did have a lot on her plate with two infants. It was possible—

Mason's phone vibrated, startling him even though he'd been waiting and checking. He stared at the Caller ID for a moment, immobilized.

"For Pete's sake, answer it," his mother urged, nudging him out of his daze.

He did, assured the caller that he was Mason Blackburne, then listened while the information was explained to him. "You're sure?"

They were completely confident in the results. Mason thanked the caller and pressed the off button on his phone.

Flo stared at him anxious and expectant. "Well? Mason, I'm too old for this kind of suspense. Don't make me wait—"

"They're mine," he said simply.

His voice was so calm and controlled when he was anything but. He was a father!

It was a shock to hear the news he'd hoped for but shocks seemed to be just another day in the ER for him these days. Images flashed through his mind of meeting Jessica the day his divorce was final. She'd sat next to him at the bar. He really had only wanted to talk. A distraction from the fact that his carefully constructed life had fallen apart.

For a while talking was all she'd done, telling him about her sister, Annie, living with her between jobs, and that he would like her. Then she'd flirted and charmed her way into his bed. He'd had a rough time of it and she promised sex without complications.

Surprise! Let the complications begin. Oddly enough, complication number one was Annie Campbell.

At least this time Mason called to ask Annie if he could come by. He'd gotten the news from the lab just like she had, so of course she agreed to see him. The problem was now she had to see him.

He was the twins' father, which gave him every right to be a part of their lives. But he made her nervous. Not

in a creepy way. More like the cute-guy-at-school-you-
had-a-crush-on kind of thing. And she had to figure out
how to co-parent with a complete stranger who made her
insides quiver like Jell-O.

There was a knock on the door. She noticed he didn't
ring the doorbell again, which meant he was capable of
learning. And it was a good thing, too, since the babies
were asleep at the same time. Although not for long since
they needed to eat.

Annie opened the door and Mason stood there, this
time in worn jeans and a cotton, button-up shirt with the
long sleeves rolled to mid-forearm. The look did nothing
to settle her nerves.

"Come in," she said without offering a hello.

But neither did Mason. He walked past her, mumbling
something about needing to buy a minivan and save for
college.

"I suppose that means you don't want to sign away
your rights as a father."

"No." His expression was intense, serious. "In fact,
since I last saw you, I consulted an attorney."

Words to put fear into a girl's heart. "I'm their legal
guardian. If you try and take them away from me—"

"Whoa." He put his hands up in a slow-down motion.
"It's just that even though I'm their father, I have no rights
because my name isn't on the birth certificate. Now, with
DNA proof, I will acknowledge paternity and petition the
court to legally claim my paternal rights."

"How long will that take?"

"There's a sixty-day waiting period, then however long
it takes to get a court date," he said.

"And then you're going to sue for sole custody?"

"Of course not. No one is talking custody fight here.
You clearly love them."

"I do. But how can you know that?" Where men were concerned, suspicion was her default emotion.

"Because you did copious research on a pacifier. And I just get the feeling that if I look at either baby funny, you'd cut my heart out with a spoon."

"You're not wrong." But how did he know her so well? They'd barely met. "Is that a negative critique on my mothering instincts?"

"Absolutely not. You're protective. And I think that's a plus. I happen to strongly believe in traditional two-parent families. That kind of environment is a positive influence in shaping their lives. It's the way I grew up and I didn't turn out so bad. I'd like my children to have that, too."

"I see." That was good, right? It was something she'd never had and desperately wanted. Especially for the twins she loved so much.

He looked around. "It's awfully quiet. Are the babies here?"

She wanted to say, "Duh." Where else would they be? There was no family to help her out. She'd barely heard from her mother and stepfather after they'd moved to the other side of the country. Jess was all she'd had. But there was no reason to be snarky to Mason.

"They're both asleep at the same time. It's a very rare occurrence." His grin made her want to fan herself but she managed to hold back.

"Maybe we should have a parade in their honor," he teased.

"Good grief, no. The marching bands would wake them up and I want to enjoy every moment of this quiet for as long as it lasts."

"Good point. A better use of this time would be for you and I to get to know each other."

He probably wouldn't like what she had to say.

Chapter Two

Annie tried to think of a reason getting to know Mason was a bad idea. She wondered how Mr. I Had a Perfect Childhood would feel about co-parenting with someone whose story wasn't so pretty. But he had a right to know.

Common sense dictated that she find out everything possible about her babies' father and she couldn't do that without giving him information about herself. But he made her nervous. To reveal her nerves would require an explanation about why that was and she didn't think she could put it into words. At least not in a rational way. Last time he'd been here, he was less than pleased about not being informed that he might be a father. Annie couldn't really blame him and wondered if he was still resentful.

"Getting to know each other is probably a good idea," she agreed. "I was going to have a quick bite to eat while Charlie and Sarah are sleeping. It's just leftovers but you're welcome to join me."

"Thanks. What can I do to help?"

"Set the table, I guess." She wasn't used to having help; it was nice. "I'm going to throw together a salad and

I have cold fried chicken. I'll nuke some macaroni and cheese." She pointed out the cupboard with the plates and the drawer containing utensils. Napkins were a no-brainer, right in plain sight in a holder on her circular oak table.

"Yes, ma'am."

"One thing about me you should know right now," Annie said as she put prewashed, bagged lettuce into a bowl. "Never call me 'ma'am.' It makes me feel like I need help crossing the street."

"Understood." He set two plates on the table. "So what should I call you? Miss Campbell?"

"Annie works." She put dressing on the greens and handed him the bowl containing long-handled serving spoons. "Toss this, please."

"Yes, ma—" He looked sheepish. "Sorry. I'm a civilian now."

"I guess you can take the man out of the military but you can't take the military out of the man." She felt a little zing in her chest when she looked at him and struggled for something to say. "So, you were in the army."

"Yes. I enlisted."

She put a casserole dish in the microwave and pushed the reheat button. "Why?"

"I wanted to go to medical school and couldn't afford it. My parents wanted to help, but it's a steep price tag and I didn't want them taking out a second mortgage or going into debt. It was the best way to get where I wanted to go without putting a strain on them. When I got my MD, I owed the military four years. The upside is that I was able to serve my country while paying back the government."

Watching him toss the heck out of that lettuce, Annie realized a couple of things. He was way above average-looking and it wasn't as hard to talk to him as she'd thought. Although, he was the one doing the talking. With a little luck he wouldn't notice that she hadn't revealed anything about herself yet.

Keep the conversation on him. She could do this. She was a grown woman now, not the geeky loner she'd once been. "So now you're a doctor."

"That's the rumor. Also known as an emergency medical specialist." He stopped tossing the salad. "I've started my job at Huntington Hills Memorial Hospital. Just so you know I'm not a deadbeat dad."

"I didn't think you were."

"Just wanted to clarify." He shrugged his broad shoulders. "This kind of feels like a job interview. Maybe the most important one I'll ever have."

"I hadn't thought about it that way. And it doesn't matter what I think," she said. "You are their biological father. Time will tell if you can be a dad."

The expression on his face didn't exactly change but his eyes turned a darker navy blue, possibly with disapproval. "Spoken like a true skeptic."

"I am and there are reasons."

"You're not the only one. Your sister wasn't going to tell me I'm a father."

Annie got his meaning. He was wondering if keeping the truth from a man was a shared family trait. Part of her wanted to remind him she was the reason her sister made the daddy candidate list. Part of her respected his skepticism about her. More often than not people let you down and the only way to protect yourself was to expect the worst. So, yay him.

"That was wrong of Jessica. In her defense, I'd like to point out that she was taking steps to do the right thing. It's not her fault that she couldn't see it through."

"Look, Annie, I didn't mean—"

"Sure you did," she interrupted. "And you're not wrong.

So this isn't a job interview as much as it's about finding a way to work together for the sake of those babies."

He thought for a moment. "Can't argue with that."

"Okay." The microwave beeped so she pulled out the casserole dish and stirred the macaroni and cheese, then put it back in for another minute. "So you have family here in Huntington Hills?"

"Parents and siblings," he confirmed.

"How many siblings?"

"Two brothers and a sister."

Annie felt the loss of her sister every day and not just because of caring for the twins. No one knew her like Jess had. They'd shared the same crappy childhood and her big sis had run interference at home and at school. She'd always had Annie's back—no matter what.

"You're lucky to have a big family."

"I know you're right, but I'm looking forward to having a place of my own," he said.

"Don't tell me." She grinned. "You're a man in his thirties living with his mother. You know what they say about that."

"No. And I don't want to know. Besides, it's not as bad as you make it sound." He smiled and the corners of his eyes crinkled in an appealing way.

"There's no way to make it sound good."

"I guess technically I live with my parents here in town. I sold my house before going to Afghanistan. I'm just staying with the folks until I can find a place of my own." His smile disappeared and there was a shadow in his eyes, something he wasn't saying.

And she didn't ask. The microwave beeped again and she retrieved the dish and set it on the table. "Okay, then. That makes it a whole lot less weird."

"Good."

"Dinner is served."

They sat across from each other and filled their plates. Well, he did. A couple pieces of chicken with a healthy portion of macaroni and cheese. He dug in as if he hadn't eaten in a week.

He finished a piece of chicken and set the bone on his plate. "So, what about you?"

"Me?"

"Yeah. I've monopolized the conversation. Now it's your turn."

She really didn't like talking about herself. "What do you want to know?"

"Do you have a job?"

"Other than caring for the twins?" She realized he had no frame of reference yet for how that was a full-time job. "I'm a graphic designer."

"I see." There was a blank look in his eyes.

"You have no idea what I do, right?"

"Not a clue," he admitted. "I was going to wait until you were busy with something else and Google it on my phone."

He was honest, she thought. That was refreshing. "Let me save you the trouble. I create a visual concept, either with computer software or sketches by hand, to communicate an idea."

"So, advertising."

"Yes. But more. Clients are looking for an overall lay-out and production design for brochures, magazines and corporate reports, too."

"So, you're artistic."

"Beauty is in the eye of the beholder, I guess. But I can honestly say that I've always loved to draw." She didn't have to tell him she was dyslexic and that made anything to do with reading a challenge. Was it genetic? He might need to know at some point but that time wasn't now. "Fortunately, I can do a lot of work from home. Which means I haven't had to leave Charlie and Sarah much. Yet."

"Oh?" He had finished off his second piece of chicken and half a helping of the macaroni. Now he spooned salad onto his plate and started on that.

Annie pushed the food around hers. Talking about herself made her appetite disappear. "We're developing an advertising package and bid for a very large and well-known company. I won't jinx it by telling you who. But if we get it, my workload could increase significantly and that would mean meetings in the office." She speared a piece of lettuce with her fork, a little more forcefully than necessary. "And the twins don't really have much to add to the discussion yet."

"What are you going to do?"

"I'm planning to cross that bridge if and when it needs crossing."

She put a brave and confident note in her voice because she didn't feel especially brave or confident. Leaving her babies with a trusted friend who bailed her out in an emergency was one thing. Turning them over to a stranger, even a seasoned child-care professional who'd passed a thorough background check was something she dreaded.

"It's really something," he said. "Taking in two infants."

"How could I not?" Annie swallowed the lump of emotion in her throat. "Their mother was my sister."

"Still, I know people who wouldn't do it. You and Jessica must have been close."

"We were. She was always there for me. No matter what—" Unexpectedly, tears filled her eyes and Annie didn't want him to see.

She stood, picked up her plate and turned away before walking over to the sink. She felt more than heard Mason come up behind her. Warmth from his body and the subtle scent of his aftershave surrounded her in a really nice way.

"Annie, if I haven't said it already, I'm very sorry for your loss."

"That's exactly what her doctor said to me when he told me she was dead. Is there a class in med school on how to break bad news to loved ones?"

"No. Unfortunately, it's just experience. The kind no doctor wants to get."

It had been three months since Jess died. Annie had thought she was out of tears and didn't want to show weakness in front of this man. Maybe because he was the babies' biological father and had a stronger and more intimate connection to them than she did. The reason didn't matter because she couldn't hold back her shaky breaths any more than she could hide the silent sobs that shook her whole body.

The next thing she knew, his big, strong hands settled gently on her upper arms and he turned her toward him, pulled her against his chest in a comforting embrace. He didn't say anything, just held her. It felt nice. And safe.

That was a feeling Annie had very little experience with in her life. Odd that it came from a relative stranger. Maybe Jess had felt it, too.

Annie got her emotions under control and took a step back. She was embarrassed and couldn't quite meet his gaze. "I'm sorry you had to see that."

"Don't be."

She shrugged. "Can't help it. I don't know why I broke down now. It's not a fresh reality."

"Maybe you haven't had time to grieve. What with suddenly being responsible for two babies."

That actually made a lot of sense to her. "Anyway, thanks."

"You're welcome. I hope it helped." He looked like he sincerely meant that. Apparently the business of helping people was the right one for him.

"Speaking of those babies, I'm going to check on them. It's not their habit to be so quiet and cooperative when I'm having a meal." The first one with their father, she noted.

"You cooked, so I'll do the dishes."

"Cook is a very nebulous term for the way I warmed up leftovers. But I'm taking that deal," she agreed.

The best one she'd had in a long time. She went to the "nursery" and found Charlie and Sarah awake and playing. Standing where they couldn't see her, she watched them exploring fingers and feet and smiling at each other.

Her heart was so full of love for these two tiny humans that it hurt, and was something she experienced daily. But having a man in her kitchen doing dishes didn't happen on a regular basis.

She found herself actually liking Mason Blackburne. So far. But she hadn't known him very long. There was still time for him to screw up and she had every confidence that he would.

Men couldn't seem to help themselves.

Mason was feeding a bottle to Charlie when he heard footsteps coming up the outside stairs followed by the apartment door opening. Annie walked in and looked at him then glanced around.

"Wow, it's quiet in here. And really neat." Was there the tiniest bit of envy in her expression? "I'm feeling a little inadequate because I can't seem to manage two infants and an apartment without leaving a trail of debris and destruction in my wake."

"Oh, well, you know—"

After several weeks of him visiting the babies every chance he could, she'd reluctantly accepted his offer to watch them while she went to her office for a meeting. He wasn't completely sure she hadn't done a background check on him before agreeing. Fortunately he'd already passed the diaper-changing, bottle-feeding and burping tests. Still, Annie had been very obviously conflicted about walking out the door and leaving him in charge. He'd assured her there was nothing to worry about and shooed her off to work.

She'd barely been gone five minutes before all hell had broken loose. Two code browns and a simultaneous red alert on the hunger front. His situational readiness went to DEFCON 1 and he'd done what he'd had to do.

Glancing at the hallway then at her, he said, "I thought you'd be gone longer."

She walked over and kissed Charlie's forehead. The scent of her skin wrapped around Mason as if she'd touched him, too, and he found himself wishing she had. The night she'd cried and he held her in his arms was never far from his mind. She'd felt good there, soft and sweet.

"I stayed for the high points then ducked out of the meeting. I just missed my babies and didn't want to be away from them any longer," she said. "How did it go? Where's Sarah?"

At that moment his mother walked into the room holding the baby in question. Florence Blackburne was inching toward sixty but looked ten years younger. Her brown hair, straight and turned under just shy of her shoulders, was shot with highlights. He'd been about to tell Annie that he'd called her for help, but he was outed now.

"You must be Annie. I'm Florence, Mason's mother."

Annie's hazel eyes opened wide when she looked at him. "I thought you said you could handle everything."

"When I said that, the ratio of adults to babies was one to one. And I did handle it," he said defensively. "I called for reinforcements." He set the bottle on the coffee table and lifted Charlie to his shoulder to coax a burp out of him. It came almost instantly, loud and with spit-up. "That's my boy," he said proudly.

"Seriously?" she said.

"Eventually he'll learn to say excuse me." Mason shrugged then returned to the subject of calling his mom. "I admit that I underestimated my multitasking abilities."

"Oh, please," Flo said. "You just couldn't stand that one of your children was unhappy."

"Yeah, there's that," he acknowledged.

"Even though I told him that crying isn't a bad thing. They'd be fine." Flo was talking to Annie now. "You know this already. You've been doing it by yourself since these little sweethearts were born."

"I have." Annie gave him a look that could mean anything from "You're a child-care jackass" to "Finally someone gets it."

"How nice that you had backup on your first solo mission."

Flo's blue eyes brimmed with sympathy and understanding as only another mother's could. She handed the baby girl to Annie. "You're not alone now, honey. Being a mother is the hardest job you'll ever do times two. And sometimes you need a break. Recharge your batteries. Take a deep breath. Go get your hair trimmed or a pedicure. I just want you to know that I'm here. Don't hesitate to call."

"I would never impose," Annie said.

"These are my grandchildren. It wouldn't be an imposition. I have a part-time job as a receptionist in a dermatology office and my hours are flexible, so we can work around that. Mason will give you my number."

"Thank you." Annie kissed Sarah's cheek. "I appreciate that."

"What are grandmothers for?" She shrugged. "Full disclosure, I might spoil them just a little because I've waited a long time to play the grandmother card. Charlie and Sarah will learn that my house is different, but I will never compromise your rules. I might be prejudiced, but these are the most beautiful babies I've ever seen. Although I don't see much of Mason in them."

"Gee, thanks, Ma," he teased.

"I didn't mean it like that, son." She smiled at him. "It's just that they look a lot like you, Annie."

She pressed her cheek to baby Sarah's. "There was a strong resemblance between my sister and me."

"Then she was very beautiful," his mom said.

"She was," Annie agreed.

The subtext was that Annie was beautiful, too, and Mason couldn't agree more. Today she was professionally dressed in slacks, a silky white blouse and black sweater. Low-heeled pumps completed the outfit, but he missed her bare feet. Her straight, silky blond hair fell past her shoulders and she was wearing makeup for the first time since he'd met her. And he'd been right. She was a knockout.

"Well, you two, now that everything is under control, I'll be going." Florence grabbed her purse, kissed Mason on the cheek and smiled fondly at her grandbabies. "It was wonderful to meet you, Annie. You don't need my approval, but it has to be said that you've done a remarkable job with your children. And I sincerely meant what I said. Call me if you need anything."

"Thank you, Mrs. Blackburne—"

"It's Flo." She patted Annie's shoulder. "'Bye."

And then the two of them were alone, each holding a baby, and Mason wondered what Annie was thinking.

"So that was my mom."

"You have her eyes."

He'd heard that before. "It turns out that when one of my children is crying because he or she has needs that I can't instantly meet, it's not something I manage very well."

"As flaws go, it's not an exceptionally bad one to have," she conceded. "So you called your mom."

"Yeah."

"And if I got home later and your mom was gone, would you have let me believe you sailed through your first time alone with them trouble free?"

He would have wanted to. There was the whole male pride thing, after all. But… "No. I'd have told you she'd been here."

"Why?"

"Because that's the truth and it's the right thing to do." He shrugged and a dozing Charlie squirmed a little against his shoulder.

"I'm not sure I believe you."

He remembered her saying she was a skeptic and had her reasons. Skepticism was rearing its ugly head now. "In time you'll be convinced that I embrace the motto that cheaters never prosper."

"And in time, if I'm convinced, something tells me your mom is responsible for that honest streak."

"Oh?"

"Yeah. She's really something."

"She's just excited and happy to finally have even one grandchild. In her world twins is winning the lottery."

"I didn't mean that as a criticism." There was a baby

quilt on the sofa beside him. Annie took it and spread the
material on the floor in front of the coffee table. She put
Sarah on it then sat next to him. "I meant just the opposite.
She's full of energy in the best possible way. The kind of
supportive, protective mother I wish my mom had been.
The kind I want to be."

That little kernel of information reminded Mason that
he didn't know much about her. The night they'd been
getting acquainted he'd given her some facts about himself. She'd only offered up what she did for a living and
then he'd held her when she'd cried. He hadn't been able
to focus on much besides the soft curves of her body and
hadn't noticed how little he'd learned. Now he was becoming aware of how guarded she was. And it wasn't just
about protecting Charlie and Sarah. She held parts of herself back and he wondered why.

He stood with Charlie in his arms, then moved to the
blanket on the floor and gently settled the sleeping baby
next to his sister. After stretching his cramped muscles,
he met Annie's gaze. "So, what you just said implies that
your mother wasn't supportive."

"She had issues."

He waited for more but that was it. "Had? Does that
mean she passed away?"

"No. She lives in Florida with her husband." When
Sarah let out a whimper, Annie jumped up as if she'd just
been waiting for an excuse to end this conversation. "Did
she have a bottle?"

"No."

"Okay." Annie scooped up the baby and went into the
kitchen to get a bottle from the refrigerator.

Mason didn't claim to be a specialist in the area of feelings but it didn't take a genius to see that Annie wasn't
comfortable talking about herself. Either she was hiding

something or there was a lot of pain in the memories. So now he knew she was a graphic artist, had adored her sister and missed her terribly. And there was stuff in her past that she didn't want to talk about.

That was okay. She was the mother of his children and he wasn't going anywhere. In his experience as an ER doc, he'd learned that often people held things back but eventually the facts came out. And he wanted all the facts about his children's legal guardian.

Chapter Three

Several weeks after Mason walked into her life Annie got her first really powerful blast of mom guilt. There had been some minor brushes with the feeling, but this one was a doozy.

Because of him, and by extension his mother, Florence, everything had changed. For the better, she admitted. The woman was fantastic with the twins so when she'd offered to watch them while Annie went to a mandatory meeting in the office, she'd gratefully accepted.

It had only been a few hours ago that Annie had walked out of her apartment but it felt like days. She checked her phone to make sure there were no messages. The empty screen mocked her and she felt the tiniest bit disposable, followed by easily replaceable. There was a healthy dose of exhilaration for this unexpected independence mixed with missing her babies terribly. The verdict was in. She was officially conflicted and on the cusp of crazy.

If all that wasn't guilt-inducing enough, she was going to have a grown-up girlfriend lunch. She should call it off and go be with Charlie and Sarah. Even as that thought popped into her head, she saw Carla Kellerman walking toward her with a food bag. Her friend had stopped to pick up something, as promised. So if Annie bugged out now, Carla would be inconvenienced. She would just have to eat fast.

"Hi." Carla came into her cubicle and smiled.

This woman was completely adorable. Perky and shiny. Straight, thick red hair fell past her shoulders and went perfectly with her warm brown eyes. She had the biggest, friendliest smile ever. And a soft, mushy heart. The occasional loss of her temper was almost always on someone else's behalf and made her completely human. As flaws went, it was adorable.

"I forgot how much I love this office," her friend said, looking around. "If I didn't already have a job, I would want to work here."

C&J Graphic Design occupied the top floor of an office building on the corner of C Street and Jones Boulevard in the center of Huntington Hills. The light wood floor stretched from the boss's office at one end of the long, narrow room to the employees' lounge at the other. Overhead track lighting illuminated cubicles separated by glass partitions. The environment had a collaborative vibe and Annie loved seeing her coworkers' creative ideas and them having easy access to hers.

"Hi, yourself." Her stomach growled. Loud.

"Apparently my arrival with provisions isn't a moment too soon." Carla grinned. "I guess I don't have to ask if you're ready to eat."

"Follow me. There are drinks in the break room fridge. Or we could sit outside." It was October but Southern California was still warm. There was a patio with wrought iron tables and chairs shaded by trees and surrounded with grass, shrubs and flowers.

"That. Door number two," her friend said. "I need fresh air."

They grabbed drinks, walked to the elevator and Annie hit the down button.

"Maybe we should go wild today and take the stairs," Carla suggested. "I could use the exercise."

"Since when? Don't get me wrong," Annie added. "I'm a supportive friend who will follow you bravely down eight flights of stairs. But this switch from 'I can't stand sweat' to 'We should take the stairs' is different."

"Not really. I always think about it."

Annie opened the stairway door and they started down. "But I can't read your mind. You never said anything before. What's changed? Got a crush on the boss?"

"Hardly. I work for Lillian Gordon."

"I know. But didn't her nephew come in to help the company over a rough financial patch?"

"Yes. Gabriel Blackburne. But he's kind of a hermit. Keeps to his office, hunched over a computer, presumably strategizing how to turn the company around."

They'd reached the ground floor and both of them were breathing a little harder as they headed for the rear door that led to the patio.

Carla gave her a look. "You have the strangest expression on your face. Why?"

"Because Mason's last name is Blackburne."

"Who's Mason?"

"The babies' father," Annie clarified.

"Small world," her friend said. "We needed this lunch even more than I thought so you can fill me in."

"I wonder if Mason is related to your Gabriel Blackburne. It's not that common a name," Annie said.

"I guess it's possible." Her friend moved decisively to the table with the most shade, put the bag down on it and sat in one of the sturdy metal chairs. "From what Lillian tells me, Gabriel is not a fan of her business plan but he does approve of the branding campaign C&J did for Make Me a Match."

"Well, he sounds a little intimidating, but definitely has good taste in graphic design companies." Annie sat at a right angle to her friend. "You'd expect Mason to be that way, but he's not."

Carla pulled two paper-wrapped sandwiches and napkins from the bag. She handed one over. "I need details. A text saying 'twins' father showed up and DNA confirms' isn't much information."

"I haven't had much time in the last few months."

"Two babies. I get it. And you're a saint, by the way. So tell me everything."

Annie explained about contacting the men Jessica thought could be the father and Mason showing up last. "He's an army doctor just back from Afghanistan. So, military and medical."

Carla took a bite of her turkey sub and chewed thoughtfully before swallowing. "He sounds honorable to me. I haven't known you long but I'm learning that you're good at finding flaws."

Not so far, Annie thought. "You know me pretty well. I'm not holding my breath he'll stay honorable. For now he's good with Charlie and Sarah. Not too proud to ask for help. The first time I left him alone with them, he called his mom for backup." Annie wasn't sure why, but she'd believed him when he'd said he wouldn't have let her think he handled the twins without a problem. "Florence, his mom, is fantastic. Loves kids and thrilled to be a grandmother. She has them now."

"Lillian's sister is Florence. Has to be the same family," her friend concluded. "Like I said, small world."

"No kidding. If Gabriel looks anything like Mason, I can see why you think you could use the exercise."

"He's pretty, but a little too dark and brooding for me. Besides, he keeps reminding everyone that he's only there temporarily." Carla shrugged. "So the twins' father is a hottie? It could be a reality show—*Real Hotties of Huntington Hills.*"

Annie laughed then thoughtfully chewed a bite of her sandwich. "'Hottie' would be an accurate description."

"You like him." Carla's voice had a "gotcha" tone.

"Why in the world would you come to that conclusion from what I just said?"

"Good question," Carla mused. "Maybe the way you were so deliberately aloof."

It was a little scary how well this woman knew her, Annie thought. They'd hit it off when working together on the branding campaign for Make Me a Match. Annie had spent some time in their office to get a feel for the dating service but the nephew had never poked his head out of his inner sanctum. Her friendship with Carla was relatively new but her assessment of Annie's feelings about Mason wasn't too far off the mark. Still, an attraction was no reason to be giddy. Just the opposite, in fact.

"It doesn't matter whether or not I like him. Men are notoriously unreliable."

"You know I agree with you about that." Carla ate the last of her sandwich then wiped her hands on a napkin. "I know we're fairly new friends and this is probably invading your privacy. Feel free to say it's none of my business, but what's your story? Why are you commitment averse?"

"Let's call it daddy issues. And before you ask, it's both biological and step. My mother has terrible taste in men. And you already know about Dwayne." Her ex-boyfriend. The jerk had sworn to always have her back but couldn't get away fast enough when she'd become the twins' legal guardian and brought them home. "I'm not going to be complacent and starry-eyed then get blind-sided when Mason decides he can't handle being a father to twins. I can only deal with one day at a time and for now he's doing all the right things."

"Like what?" Carla asked.

"Well…" Annie thought for a moment and fought a smile she knew would look tender and goofy. "Hardly a day has gone by that he hasn't come to see them. He said he's already lost too much time being their father and doesn't want to miss another single moment with his kids that he doesn't absolutely have to."

"How sweet is that? Certainly not the behavior of a man who's going to abandon them," Carla pointed out.

"Maybe." It was hard to argue with that assertion so Annie didn't. "He works in the emergency room at Huntington Hills hospital and he looks so tired sometimes it's a wonder he can stand up, let alone hold one of the babies."

"Wow." Carla stared at her in disbelief. "Do you have recent pictures of the twins?"

"What kind of mom would I be if I didn't?" Annie proudly pulled a cell phone out of her slacks' pocket, found the most recent photos and then handed it over so her friend could scroll through.

"The twins are beautiful. And I say again—wow." Carla's eyebrows went up. "He's such a cutie, and I'm not talking about Charlie. This one of Mason holding both babies is a seriously 'aww moment.'"

Annie glanced at the picture and smiled at the memory of Mason dozing off while they were on his chest. He held them securely in place with a big hand on each of their backs. The moment did have a serious cuteness quotient, which was why she'd taken the photo. "More than once he's fallen asleep on my sofa."

"Oh?"

"Down girl." She hadn't been able to resist snapping the picture, but it didn't mean anything. Certainly not that she was looking at the future. One day at a time worked just fine for her. "Naps on my couch are about a demanding career, work schedule and his children," Annie said. "It has nothing to do with me. Or us."

"Still, he's not a troll and he likes kids. That's a good start."

"There is no start," Annie argued. "How can there be when he doubts my character? He made it clear that he doesn't trust me."

"What does he have against you? The two of you just met."

"He was justifiably curious about why my sister didn't contact him when she found out she was pregnant, about the possibility that he was a father. I got the feeling that, with him, that lie of omission extended to me because I'm Jessica's sister."

"Is it possible that you're inventing reasons to push him away? Like I said, you're good at finding flaws," Carla said. "Does it bother you that Jessica slept with him first?"

"Of course not. And, as you pointed out, I just met him a few weeks ago." Annie analyzed the question a little deeper. "And by *first* you're suggesting that I will sleep with him, too. That's just not going to happen."

Carla shrugged. "If you say so."

"You're seeing a relationship where none exists. Is Lillian working you too hard at Make Me a Match?" Annie teased. "Maybe you can't leave work at the office?"

Her friend laughed ruefully. "We need satisfied customers. And they need to spread the word about the valuable service we provide if the business is going to survive."

"I'll talk it up and, if I can, send clients your way," Annie promised.

But she wouldn't be one of them. She had enough on her hands without falling in love. Lust was a different thing altogether and had a mind of its own. Proof of that was the vision of twisted sheets and strong arms that had been keeping her awake at night. And those arms didn't belong to just anyone. They were definitely Mason's.

Mason was at the apartment with the twins several days after his mom had watched them. Annie was putting in more hours at her office because the deadline for the high-profile campaign was approaching fast. He'd gotten Sarah to sleep and had spent the last fifteen minutes walking Charlie. Now he carefully lifted the baby from his shoulder and put him on his back in the crib, beside his sister. He held his breath, fingers crossed that the little boy was finally sound enough asleep that the movement wouldn't wake him. No sound, no movement. Mission objective achieved.

He looked down at them—his children—and thought for the billionth time how beautiful and perfect they were. And how lucky he was to have them. Sure, he hadn't known from the beginning about the pregnancy and could whine about that, but it wouldn't have changed anything. A lot of active-duty service members missed out on big family moments because of deployment. The truth was, he couldn't have been there for their birth even if he'd known.

So he hadn't been able to support Annie through the shock and sadness of losing her sister. A little extra help with the babies wouldn't have hurt, either. Somehow she'd had the strength to do it all by herself. On the other hand, he wouldn't be going through the legal maze of securing his paternal rights now if things had been different.

It had been a month since he'd stood at Annie's door for the first time and he could hardly remember a life without his kids—and her—in it. He'd seen the commercials on TV for companies that facilitated meets for people who wanted a relationship. The tagline: Never More Ready to Fall in Love. Mason was the opposite of that. Never less ready for love.

The collapse of his marriage had been a horrible warning. He found out that even if one made all the right moves and everything was perfect, it was still possible to fail spectacularly. And painfully. Because of things out of his control. He wouldn't make the same mistake.

That didn't mean he couldn't be in awe of Annie Campbell. He thought about her more than he liked, even when he was slammed with patients in the emergency room. She was quite a woman—sexy, beautiful, maternal, funny and smart. Everything a man could want. So why hadn't a guy snatched her up?

The doorbell rang and he swore under his breath, then checked the babies for any sign it woke them. Neither moved so he hurried to the front door, ready to chew out whoever had been stupid enough to ignore the baby sleeping sign.

He opened the door and saw a thirty-something guy standing there. He was well dressed and nice-looking. Mason wanted to strangle him. "Can you read?"

"What?"

"Did you see the sign?" He pointed. "The babies are sleeping."

"Right. Sorry, man. I forgot."

"How to read?" Now he really wanted to strangle this guy.

"No. That the babies are here." He held out his hand. "Dwayne Beller."

Mason hesitated then shook hands. "Mason Blackburne."

"The father?"

"Of the twins? Yeah." Now his curiosity was on high alert. "Who are you?"

"Annie's boyfriend." He shifted uncomfortably. "At least, I was."

"So you're not now?"

"No."

Mason felt an odd sort of relief that she was no longer with this guy. "What happened?"

"Is Annie here?"

"No." He stood feet apart, blocking the doorway.

"Do you mind telling me where she is?"

"Yes." They were sizing each other up. "Mind telling me what happened with you and Annie?"

Dwayne shifted his stance uncomfortably. "Look, man, would you just tell her I stopped by?"

"Why?"

"Because I'd like her to know that I was here."

Mason didn't miss the fact that Dwayne was looking pretty irritated. It didn't bother him at all. "I meant why don't you want to talk about what happened?"

"Because it's none of your business. It's between Annie and me—"

"Dwayne?" Annie was almost at the top of the stairs and her eyes widened at the scene unfolding in front of her door.

She had several bags of groceries in her hands and didn't look happy to see the guy. That didn't bother Mason at all, either.

"Hi, Annie. You look good." The ex-boyfriend had a sheepish expression on his face and glanced at Mason, who was still blocking the door. "Can I come in?"

"Why?" she asked warily.

"To talk," he said. "I really miss talking to you."

There was hurt and disillusionment in her eyes, proof the line wasn't working. "I don't think there's anything left for us to say to each other."

"Please just hear me out."

"These bags are getting heavy." She elbowed past him and Mason stepped aside to let her through. "And you said quite enough the last time I saw you. At Jessica's memorial service. Your timing left a lot to be desired."

Dwayne elbowed his way past Mason and followed her into the apartment, watching her set bags on the table. "Look, Annie, that wasn't my finest hour. I admit it, but—"

"There's no but," she snapped. "At the worst time in my life you walked out on me. That doesn't deserve a but."

"No one feels worse about that than me." The jerk held out his hand, a pleading gesture. "The thought of being a father freaked me out, okay? Two at once is a lot."

"Yeah, tell me about it." Her tone dripped sarcasm.

"You were distracted and I was starting to wonder if you were ever going to be there for me. For us. But I've had time to think. I miss you. I can't forget you."

Mason could understand that. Annie was unforgettable and this idiot had voluntarily walked out on her. The last thing he should get was a do-over.

Fortunately she appeared unmoved by his words. "Honestly, I haven't had time to think about you at all, what with two infants to take care of. The fact is, you never cross my mind. In case that's not clear enough, there is not a snowball's chance in hell I would ever consider taking you back. You abandoned me once. I won't give you a chance to do that to me again."

"I wish you'd reconsider. We were good together. At home and at work."

Dwayne must be desperate, Mason thought. After what she'd just said it was clear she'd made up her mind.

Annie's eyes narrowed. "Oh, now I get it. And the verdict is official. You're a conniving weasel dog and I don't ever want to see you again."

"Annie, please. I really need this—"

"Oh? I needed you," she said. "And you couldn't get out of here fast enough then. I'd like you to do that now. Just go."

"Annie—"

Mason had seen enough. He moved next to her. "The lady asked you to leave."

Dwayne's ingratiating performance disappeared. "What are you going to do? Throw me out?"

"If I have to." Mason stared at him and knew the exact moment the moron realized it was over.

"Your loss, Annie. Remember that."

"In my opinion, I dodged a bullet," she snapped back.

Without another word, the creep left and slammed the door. Hard.

Mason and Annie looked at each other and said at the same time, "The babies."

They hurried down the hall to check on them but Charlie and Sarah were still sleeping soundly. In unison, they heaved a sigh of parental relief then quietly backed out of the room and returned to the kitchen.

She met his gaze. "So, that happened."

"He's determined. I'll give him that."

"Yeah." She closed her eyes for a moment, as if erasing any vision of Dwayne from her mind. After letting out a long breath she said, "I could have called him much worse than a weasel dog."

"Me, too, but that was pretty descriptive."

"It was a compliment compared to what I was thinking. He's lucky I didn't throw something at him."

Mason studied her face and realized he had never seen her furious. The cleansing breath she'd taken hadn't cleansed anything. There was more. "What else did he do? Besides leave you at the worst possible time."

She met his gaze. "The last thing he said before bailing on me was that raising some other guy's brats wasn't what he'd signed up for."

"Son of a bitch—" Mason felt the words like a body blow. He didn't like the guy but Annie had at one time. He couldn't imagine the scope of betrayal she'd experienced. Now he was furious, too. "Good thing you threw him out. I'd have tossed him over the railing."

Surprisingly, she laughed. "That's a very satisfying image."

"What did he mean about working well together?"

"He's a graphic artist, too. It's how we met, collaborating on a job."

So they had something in common, spoke each other's language. "And when he said he needed this? Any idea what that was about?"

"He's employed by a rival firm. My guess is that they're in competition for this big contract I've been working on. If I took him back, he'd have access to my team's creative direction and could take steps to counter in their own presentation."

"So he wanted to steal from you," he said, seething with anger.

"That's my guess."

"Prince of a guy. Just oozing integrity. Damn right you dodged a bullet."

"Wow," she said. "Don't sugarcoat it. Tell me how you really feel."

"I don't mean to hurt your feelings." That was completely sincere. He would never hurt her. Not deliberately. But he couldn't hold this back. "I just have to ask. What the hell did you ever see in that guy?"

Her hazel eyes turned more green than gold. It was a clue that he'd crossed a line. Her next words confirmed that he'd said something wrong.

High color appeared on her cheeks. "It's really easy to be on the outside looking in and draw conclusions. I've known you, what? Fifteen minutes? Yes, we share the babies and you're their father. Calling them brats makes him lower than pond scum. But I get to say that. You don't get a say about my personal life, especially for something that happened before I met you."

"Annie, I—"

She held up a hand. "Now is not a good time to talk. I have another bag of stuff to bring inside. I'll get it," she said when he was about to offer. "I'm embarrassed by what just happened and taking it out on you. I need the exercise to shake off this unreasonable reaction."

Without another word, she walked out the door. Mason let her go even though every instinct was pushing him to go after her. But moments later he heard her cry out just before a scream of pain. He rushed outside and looked down. Annie was in a heap on the cement at the bottom of the stairs.

Chapter Four

One minute Annie was walking down the stairs, the next she was falling and desperately reaching out for something to stop the downward plunge. Something stopped her, all right. It was called cement. A jarring pain shot through her right leg. She cried out just before it took her breath away. Moments later Mason was there.

"Don't move," he ordered.

"Fat chance," she managed to choke out. "Knocked the...wind out...of me."

"Where does it hurt?" He ran his hands over her head and down her body. "Did you hit your head?"

"No. My leg."

After helping her to a sitting position, he gently touched her knee and shin. Searing pain made her cry out. "Ow!"

He slid her sandal off and put two fingers on her ankle, a serious expression on his face. Apparently he noticed her questioning look because he said, "I'm checking the pulse—blood circulation."

"Why?"

"Make sure nothing is restricting it," he said.

She was almost afraid to hear the answer but asked anyway. "What would be doing that?"

"The bone."

Yup, she was right. Didn't want to know that. Then he checked her foot and dragged his thumb lightly across the arch. It tickled and she involuntarily moved, sending a sharp pain up her leg.

"Ow—" She gritted her teeth because she wanted so badly to cry.

"Do you have scissors?"

"Kitchen drawer. What are you—?"

But he was gone and she heard his footsteps racing up the stairs. He was back in less than a minute with her heavy shears in his hand. He positioned them at the hem of her slacks.

"You're going to cut them?"

"Yes. I'm concerned about swelling. They'll do it at the hospital anyway. I think your leg is broken."

"No. I don't have time for that."

He met her gaze, and his was serious and doctorly. "You're going to have to make time. I'm taking you to the hospital."

"Can't you brace it with a couple of tree branches and wrap it in strips from a dirty T-shirt?"

One corner of his mouth curved up. "You've been watching too many action shows on TV."

That was probably true. "You could be wrong. Maybe it's just a really painful sprain and you're overreacting."

"I hope I am." His serious tone said he was pretty sure that wasn't the case. "You still need an X-ray to make sure. I'm taking you to my emergency room to get it checked out."

"Oh, bother—" She closed her eyes and tried not to move and make it hurt more. "I've been up and down those stairs more than a hundred times. How did this happen?"

"My guess is you tripped over that box of disposable diapers." He pulled his cell phone from his pocket.

"Oh." Vaguely she remembered bringing bags from the car and trying to take as much as possible in one trip. Between her parking spot and the flight of steps, the box started slipping so she'd set it on one of the steps near the bottom, intending to grab it when she got the last bag. What with the Dwayne drama, she'd forgotten all about it. It was a big box because she went through a lot of diapers— "Mason, the babies!"

"It's all right. I'm calling my mom. She'll take care of them."

"But they're my responsibility—"

"And mine," he quietly reminded her. "But everyone needs help sometime, Annie. And you really don't have a choice right now."

She hated that he was right.

While they waited for his mother, he fashioned a splint from a cardboard mailing box and duct tape to immobilize her leg. Then he filled a plastic bag with ice, wrapped it in a towel and put it on the injured limb to reduce swelling. Flo got there in record time and gave Annie a quick hug and reassuring smile before hurrying up the stairs to handle the twins.

"Okay," Mason said, "let's get you to the car." He helped her stand without putting any weight on the injured leg but the movement sent pain grinding through her. There was a grim look on his face when she cried out. "I was afraid of that. Either I carry you or we call paramedics."

"No ambulance."

"That's what I thought. This will be faster and less painful. Brace yourself. Deep breath."

He gently lifted her and she slid her arms around his neck then held on. In spite of the pain, she had that familiar feeling of safety when he held her and closed her eyes while he moved as quickly as he could without jostling her too much. His SUV was at the curb in front of the complex and he got her into the rear, where she propped the bad leg up across the leather seats.

When they arrived at the emergency room entrance, someone in scrubs was waiting at the curb with a wheelchair. Mason quietly but firmly directed that she be taken to Radiology and he would meet them there with paperwork. He was as good as his word and while waiting for the X-ray tech to take her back she filled out medical forms and insurance information.

It turned out that the scrubs guy was an ER nurse who worked closely with Mason—Dr. Blackburne. He told her that Mason was smart, skilled and one of the best diagnosticians he'd ever known. Everyone liked him. And his combat medical experience saved more than one life during a recent MVA trauma—motor vehicle accident involving multiple cars and victims with critical, life-threatening injuries.

"I think this is just a bad leg sprain," Annie told him. "But Mason believes it's broken."

"Hate to say it, but he's probably right."

It turned out that he was.

After the films were taken, Mason got them to the front of the line to be read by the radiologist.

Annie was sitting on a gurney in Emergency with the curtain pulled when he came to give her the results.

"I have good news and bad," he said.

"Don't ask which I want first. Just tell me the worst," she said.

"It's broken." There was sympathy in his eyes, not the satisfaction of being right. "You'll need to be in a cast."

"How long?"

"That's up to the orthopedic doc. In a few minutes he's going to set it—"

"And plaster it?" she asked.

"Probably fiberglass. It's lighter. The goal is to control your pain and swelling, then keep it immobilized while the bone heals."

She folded her arms over her chest and frowned at him. "I see no good news in that scenario."

"It won't require surgery to set the bone."

"Does that mean I can walk on it?" she asked hopefully.

"No. Non-weight-bearing for six to eight weeks depending on how fast you heal and whether or not you follow doctor's orders."

"I'm sorry. Did you say eight weeks?"

"Max. Less if you don't push yourself too soon," he confirmed. "And, in the good news column, a broken bone heals much faster than soft tissue damage, like muscles, tendons, ligaments."

"Oddly enough, that doesn't make me feel a whole lot better. I have two four-month-old infants." This nightmare was expanding exponentially. "How am I going to take care of them? Go to the store? Walk the floor if they're crying?" Then the worst hit her. "I live in a second-floor apartment. I have to go up and down stairs. There's no elevator."

"If you put weight on it before that bone heals, there will be complications," he warned.

"So what am I supposed to do?" She was very close to

tears but not from physical discomfort, although her leg was throbbing painfully. Dyslexia had been a challenge in school and the bullying that resulted was emotionally devastating, but she'd learned coping skills. None of that had prepared her to cope with this.

"Move in with me," Mason said.

That sudden declaration kept her from crying. "Just like that? It was the first thing that popped into your head?"

"I've had time to process the situation."

She was still bitter about him being right. "Because you knew all along it was broken."

"Yes. I'm just glad it's not more serious."

"It's more serious to me."

That was self-pity, raw and unattractive. She wasn't proud of it, but couldn't deny the feeling. He probably thought she was being a drama queen, what with seeing patients who had injuries much more serious and life-threatening. But she had her babies to think about. How was she going to take care of them?

Through her shock she was trying to work out the logistics of what was happening to her. "I can work from home and have groceries delivered. But I can't hold a baby and walk on crutches. I won't be able to pick up Charlie to feed him. Or carry Sarah into the bathroom to bathe her. And it's my right leg. That will make driving difficult, if not impossible." Her heart was breaking. "How will I get them to the pediatrician? Maybe Uber…but the complications—"

"Move in with me," he repeated.

"I don't know you," she blurted.

He sighed. "Look, I know this is upsetting. But it's been a month now. Have I let you down? Have I done anything suspicious or weird?"

"You mean aside from living with your parents?"

"I haven't had a lot of time to go house hunting." He moved closer to the bed and looked down at her. "If it would make you feel better, you could do a background check."

Annie's eyes filled with tears. "I know I'm being silly. You've been terrific and your mom is a goddess. But it's hard for me to deal with the fact that I can't do this on my own."

"My parents have a single-story house and lots of room. Believe me when I say they would love it if you and their grandchildren stayed with them."

"How do you know? Have you talked to them about it?"

"As a matter of fact, I have," he said. "I would tell you if they were hesitant, but they couldn't have been more enthusiastic."

"I don't know—"

"Look, Annie, we can keep this up however long you want, but we'll end up in the same place." He sat on the bed, being careful not to crowd her injured leg, and took her hand in his big warm one. "The thing is, you don't really have a lot of options."

He was right again and she wasn't any happier about it this time. She nodded and one tear trickled down her cheek. "Okay. But only for the babies."

Mason carried the last box from Annie's apartment into her new room. She was sitting in the glider chair with her casted leg elevated on the ottoman. Charlie was sacked out in one of the cribs his parents had bought and Annie was holding a sleeping Sarah in her arms.

He'd spent his day off making trips back and forth for all the baby paraphernalia, her clothes and toiletries. In between carrying the babies to her for feeding and cuddling, he put everything away in the pine armoire and matching dresser. Using the top of it for diaper supplies, the second crib beside it was being turned into the changing table. His parents wanted their grandkids to spend a lot of time there and had insisted on buying a bed for each baby.

That meant Annie would be there, too. He liked the prospect of spending time with her, especially being under the same roof. For the next six weeks at least, he wouldn't fall asleep on that uncomfortable couch of hers.

"Hi," she said.

"Hey."

"What's in the box?"

"Toys." He set the box in a corner, out of the way. With her on crutches, the last thing he wanted was for her to trip and fall.

Two days ago he'd brought her here from the hospital and his mom had helped her care for the twins. This was his brothers' old room. It had bunk beds but was still a little crowded with Annie and the babies. Between working a shift and moving things from the apartment, Mason hadn't had a chance to talk to her. He'd missed it. He didn't want to, but it was pretty hard to ignore how glad he was to see her.

"This is the last of the things on your list. Unless you think of something else."

"You look tired," she said softly.

"Don't feel guilty."

"Who said anything about—?"

"I can hear it in your voice." Funny how he knew her that well in a relatively short period of time. "It's not your fault."

"Yeah, it kind of is," she said. "I left the box of diapers on the stairs."

"That's why it's called an accident. On the plus side, my folks are over the moon about you and the twins being here." And, though he didn't want to be, so was he.

Mason moved closer to the chair and smiled at his beautiful daughter. "How are the kids handling this change of environment?"

"It's different and they know. Not much napping going on today. I could tell they were a little restless and out of sorts." She looked up and there were shadows under her eyes, proving someone besides him was not getting enough sleep. On top of that she was pale and there were traces of pain around her mouth from the recent trauma.

"How are you holding up? Are you staying off the leg per doctor's orders?"

"Have you met your mother? She's the keep-that-leg-elevated police. If I get up for anything other than the bathroom, her feelings are hurt because I didn't ask for help." Her full lips curved upward. "She's completely fantastic, Mason. So is your dad."

"You'll get no argument from me."

"Flo must be exhausted. Basically she's been doing the work of three people, between the babies and me."

"I think she's asleep." The TV in the family room was off and the house quiet when he'd come home with the last box.

"Good." Annie nodded. "She checked in with me when you went for the last load and wanted to put Sarah in the crib for me, but I just want to hold her. Your mom, bless her, completely understood. She was turning in and wanted to make sure I didn't need anything. She said to holler if I did."

"Well, I'm back and just on the other side of the bathroom." There were entrances to it from each bedroom. "If Charlie or Sarah wakes up, I'll hear them."

Annie shifted the baby in her arms. "Can you put her in the crib for me?"

"Sure." Mason leaned down and slid his hands under the little girl and carefully lifted her. After a soft kiss on her forehead, he set her on her back beside her brother. "She's out cold. So is Charlie."

"Excellent."

"Now you can get some rest," he advised.

"Yeah." But she reached for her crutches leaning against the wall beside her. "After I take a shower."

What? He'd started out of the room and froze then turned back. "You can't get the cast wet."

"Not breaking news, Dr. Do Right. The ortho doc was very clear on that."

He could see she was determined to stand and moved the ottoman out of her way. "So it's going to be a hop-in-and-out kind of thing. Quick."

"Believe me, no one gets that better than I do." She pulled herself up awkwardly, winced with discomfort, then arranged the crutches beneath her arms. "But I'm stuck with this obnoxious thing for a while and I have to bathe."

"Of course. But my sister is off tomorrow. She's a nurse and could help you—"

"I can handle this, Mason. Don't try to talk me out of it. Another sponge bath isn't going to cut it. And I'm going to wash my hair or die trying. So get out of my way. I don't want to hurt you."

She looked fierce and beautiful and so cute. Something in his chest squeezed tight for a moment, then he laughed at the idea of a little thing like her hurting him.

She glared at him. "It's not funny. After two days, I can't stand myself."

He could stand her. A lot. What he couldn't stand was

her getting hurt. Seeing her at the bottom of the stairs had taken time off his life and he didn't want to speculate on how much. Showering on her own was a disaster in the making. She was still getting used to the crutches and learning to balance on one leg to keep her weight off the other. It wouldn't take much for this to go sideways, literally, real fast.

"Okay. At least let me help you with a strategy. Figure out the steps, pardon the pun, of this operation."

There was a suspicious gleam in her eyes. "Like what?"

"Keeping your cast dry for starters. A few drops on the outside isn't a big deal. But if you get the inside wet it can lead to a skin infection."

"That sounds pretty gross," she agreed. "So what do you have in mind?"

"I'll be back in a minute. Wait here."

"Seriously? You don't want me to hobble along and keep you company?" Letting the crutches take her weight, she stood there with a teasing look in her eyes.

"Right." He grinned then left the room.

The logistics of this maneuver ran through his mind as he hurried to the kitchen and grabbed the things he wanted. That kept him from thinking too much about Annie naked in the shower except for the lime-green cast on her leg.

Actually the vision popped into his mind anyway, along with the steadily increasing urge to kiss her. If he did, that could be a problem. Clearly she didn't trust easily and he wouldn't be another Dwayne in her life who made promises he couldn't keep.

When he came back to the bathroom, it was empty. "Annie?"

"Coming." Her soft voice came from the other side of the door. Then she shuffled back into the light wearing a short, pink terry-cloth robe, under which she probably wore nothing.

Sweat popped out on his forehead and he nearly swallowed his tongue. "I thought you were going to stay put."

"I changed out of my clothes."

"Yeah. Because that's what you do when you take a shower." He sounded like a moron. *It's what happened when blood flow from your brain rerouted to another part of your anatomy.*

"What's all that stuff for?"

Apparently she was more focused on what he'd brought than what he'd said. Good. "A plastic trash bag, duct tape and a pitcher. Sit down and I'll show you."

She moved over and sat on the closed toilet lid then rested the crutches against the sink. "Now what?"

Now he would do his level best to act professionally and not let on that he was crazy attracted to her. "I'm going to put the bag over your leg. Before I secure it with the tape, I'm going to tuck this hand towel into the top of the cast so that if the bag leaks it will still keep the inside dry."

"Great idea. I love it when a plan comes together."

Not yet, but if his hands didn't shake when he touched her, he'd call it a win.

Mason went down on one knee and put her foot on his thigh. Then he did his thing with the towel. There was no way he could avoid touching her skin and the contact just south of her thigh was sweet torture. He tried not to notice, but the material of her robe separated just a little. Not enough to get a glimpse of anything he shouldn't but enough to torment him with what he couldn't see.

He took a deep breath, as if he was going underwater, then opened the plastic bag and slid it up over her cast.

Twisting it closed just below her knee, he wrapped it securely with the tape then ripped it off the roll.

Annie nodded her approval. "That looks watertight."

"You still need to keep it away from the running water. Hang it outside the shower stall."

"What's that for?"

He glanced at the small, plastic sixteen-ounce measuring cup she was pointing to. "I'll help you wash your hair in the sink. The less time you spend in the shower, the better."

Her mouth pulled tight for a moment. "So I need to let go of a long, hot, relaxing wash."

"Like I said, it will be quick. Sorry."

"Not as sorry as I am." She met his gaze. "Let's do this."

"I'll get towels." He went to the linen closet in the hall and brought back two big fluffy ones. "This one is for your hair."

"Okay."

"Ready?"

When she nodded, Mason helped her stand, then put his hand at her waist and tried not to wish she didn't have that robe on. He instructed her to bend over the sink. Her shampoo and conditioner were right where he'd put them after unpacking her toiletries.

He turned on the water and filled the cup to wet all that beautiful blond, silky hair. He was a doctor and had been married, but this was the first time he'd ever washed a woman's hair. There was something incredibly sensual about the soapy strands running through his fingers.

No way could he stop himself from picturing her, him in the shower together with water running over their bodies. Surely he was going to hell for impure thoughts at the expense of an injured woman. He rinsed the soap as thoroughly as possible then used the conditioner and went through the same procedure, wondering if a man could go to hell twice.

"All finished." His voice was a little hoarse and with any luck she was too preoccupied to notice. He helped her straighten then handed her the towel to wrap around her hair while he steadied her. It didn't escape his notice that the pulse at the base of her neck was fluttering a little too fast. If there was any satisfaction from this ordeal at all, it was that she might be as affected by him as he was by her.

"Okay. Now for the hard part. I'll aim the showerhead away from the door so you can stick your leg out."

After he did that, she looked at him pointedly. "You can leave now."

Here was the classic definition of conflict. He wanted to get as far away from her as possible. At the same time, he didn't want to leave her and risk a fall. But the fact was he couldn't stay. He was trying to be a gentleman, not picturing her naked. The last thing he wanted was to be a sleazeball who reinforced all her reasons for being a skeptic. This might just be the hardest thing he'd ever done.

"Okay. But I'll be just on the other side of the door if you need anything."

"Thanks."

He turned his back and walked out, shutting the door behind him. That's as far as he got. He'd never forget her cry of pain when she'd fallen on the cement and hoped to God he didn't hear it now. So he waited right by that door just in case he needed to get to her in seconds.

He waited to hear the shower go on and it was a while because she had to hobble over, take off that sexy little robe, step in and set the crutches aside. The water went off fairly quickly so she'd gotten the message about not standing under it for too long.

And speaking of long, he stood in that same spot by the door for quite a while after he heard her leave the bathroom and go into the other bedroom. What the hell was wrong with him?

Stupid question. If this was a clinical situation, he would be focused on the medicine. Only that wasn't the case.

It was personal. No matter how hard he tried to stop, no matter how hard he tried not to be attracted to Annie, this was getting more personal every day.

Chapter Five

A week after breaking her leg, Annie and the kids were pretty much settled into a routine with Mason's family. He worked twelve-hour shifts for a couple of days, then was off a couple. When he was gone, his mother took over helping with the twins, bringing one or the other to Annie for feeding and cuddles. When Mason's dad, John, got home from work, he pitched in, too. His sister, Kelsey, had nursing shifts at the hospital, but happily lent a hand when she was home. It occurred to Annie to wonder why a grown man living with his parents was weird, but not a grown woman.

Mason swore that as soon as there was time he was going house hunting. And she wondered why he hadn't kept his house before he deployed to Afghanistan instead of selling it. One of these days she planned to ask him.

Right now she was too busy feeling guilty and sorry for herself. She was only good for elevating her bum leg and petting the dog while the rest of the adults took care of her babies. She could hear them in the other room getting baths. There was a lot of laughing and splashing going on and she was missing out on all the fun. Broken legs sucked.

Dogs did not. Lulu was a black shih tzu–poodle mix and completely adorable. Annie rubbed her hand over the animal's soft furry back and smiled when Lulu licked her hand, like kisses to say "Thank you for paying attention to me." When she stopped for a moment, sad brown eyes looked up at her. "Sorry, Lulu. I have to get up off this couch and go see the kids."

Florence Blackburne picked that moment to come in and check on her. "Not so fast, young-lady. Your orders are to stay off that leg as much as possible."

"But I'm missing them grow up." Annie knew she was being overly dramatic and…dare she say it? Whining? But she couldn't help it. "You don't understand."

"Maternal guilt? Boredom? Missing your children?"

"Yeah, that." The words backed Annie up a bit.

Flo sat in the club chair at a right angle to her position on the sofa. "When I was pregnant with Kelsey, my youngest, I had a condition known as placenta previa, which could cause complications during labor and delivery. I was put on bed rest until she was developed enough to take her by C-section."

"Oh, my."

"I had three small and very active boys who didn't understand why Mommy couldn't do all the things she did before. I'll never forget Mason's little face when he asked me to throw the ball with him outside and I couldn't. It broke my heart."

"How did you get through it?"

"My in-laws were fantastic. It would have been almost impossible if not for them."

"You were fortunate."

"Don't I know it. The children adored them. We all still miss them." Her voice went soft for a moment. "They died a few years ago, a couple of months apart. She went first and my father-in-law seemed in good health, except for missing her. He didn't know how to go on without her."

"He died of a broken heart," Annie commented.

Flo smiled sadly. "That's what I always thought. My family helped, too. My sister, Lillian, adored the boys and was here as much as possible on top of her full-time job."

"So you had support from both sides of the family."

"I always suspected there was a spreadsheet and schedule," the other woman said teasingly. "Lillian was in charge of that, but business and records weren't her thing. She was always a romantic and said there's nothing sexy about numbers."

Annie grinned. "That depends on who's using the algorithm."

"So I've been told," Flo said. "My son Gabriel is helping her out with her business right now and I'm told he's not hard on the eyes."

"My friend Carla works at Make Me a Match." Annie explained how they'd met. "It's not a rumor that he's a hottie. She has firsthand knowledge."

Flo grinned. "Family can be both difficult and indispensable. So, my advice is, since there's no way your broken leg is going to heal as fast as you want it to, just sit back and enjoy the help. We're happy to be doing it."

"Thank you. It's appreciated more than I can possibly say." Annie smiled when Lulu rested a paw on her left leg and whined just a little to be petted. She happily obliged. "Please don't think I'm not grateful, because I am. And maybe I'm a control freak. But I haven't had very much experience with backup."

"Do you have family?"

"My mother and her husband. Stepfather," she added.

"You don't like him." Flo wasn't asking.

"How did you know? I thought I was hiding my feelings pretty well."

"You didn't call him *your* stepfather." The woman shrugged. "No offense, but you're not a very good actress."

Sometimes Annie wished she was better at it. Like the night Mason had washed her hair and waterproofed her cast. She'd been a bundle of feelings and jumped every time his fingers had grazed her skin. Every touch was like a zing of awareness, but he probably hadn't noticed. He'd never looked at her, just concentrated on positioning duct tape.

The thing was, Annie liked when he touched her. A lot. But since he'd shown up at her apartment, there'd been no signal from him that he had the slightest personal interest, other than being a father to the twins. They had to parent together. That was all. If she let the secret of her attraction show, it would be humiliating, and her life was already filled with enough humiliation.

Annie looked at the other woman. "I don't hide my feelings well. That could be why Jess and I didn't see much of him and my mother after they moved to Florida."

"Did they know she was pregnant?" Flo asked.

Bitterness welled up inside Annie. "They knew. And they know she died after the twins were born. But they haven't seen their grandchildren even once."

Speaking of being an actress, Mason's mother couldn't or wouldn't conceal the shock and disapproval that showed on her face. "Grandchildren are our reward for not strangling our kids as teenagers. But... Never mind."

Flo seemed so open and Annie couldn't figure out why she was reluctant to say more. Just then the dog jumped off the couch and trotted to the kitchen. Moments later the doggie door slapped open and shut.

"What were you going to say?" Annie couldn't stifle her curiosity.

"I shouldn't judge people I don't know."

"But…?" She prodded.

"No. Florida is on the other side of the country. I have zero knowledge about their financial situation."

"I can tell you have an opinion," Annie nudged.

"Of course. I have opinions on everything." Flo shifted in the chair. "How's the leg? Are you comfortable?"

"I'm as comfy as possible." Annie had her leg elevated on the coffee table with the cast resting on a throw pillow. "And you're changing the subject."

"Yes." Flo sighed. "I don't want you to think I'm awful."

"Seriously?" Now it was Annie's turn to be shocked. This woman had been nothing but kind, welcoming and a godsend. "I could never think that. I can't imagine what I'd have done without this whole family and I don't even want to imagine it. I've actually thought this, so I'll just say it straight out. You're a goddess."

"Right back at you. The thing is, maybe I have strong feelings because I've waited for grandkids for quite a long time. I'd hoped Mason would…" Flo checked her words and sadness slipped into her eyes. "That was another life. It's just that I can't picture not knowing my children's children. They're a blessing."

"The babies are for me, too," Annie said.

"Thank you for sharing them with us. I just want to be included. If I overstep, you are to let me know. I mean that, Annie."

"I promise."

"If I do, just know that it comes from a place of love. I don't want to miss out on anything."

"Okay. And you should know that if I don't think to

reach out, it's nothing more than me being tired and brain-dead, certainly not deliberate. And you have to tell me."

"Thank you." Flo smiled and reached over to squeeze her hand.

Lulu returned to stand in front of Annie. The little black dog whined softly and Annie had learned this meant she wanted a treat for successfully going potty outside. The jar was beside her and she plucked out a bone-shaped biscuit, holding it just within the animal's reach. Lulu stood on her back legs, opened her mouth and snatched it from Annie's fingers then took it to her favorite spot underneath the dining room table. Annie was happy to be of use, at least to one member of this household.

But back to her folks. Annie thought about them. "My mom and stepfather have missed everything and don't seem to mind. That's in character. When I was growing up, they seemed happiest when they didn't have to get involved in mine and Jess's life."

"It's hard finding balance between hovering constantly, being a helicopter parent, and backing off to let your child's independence evolve." Flo looked as if she was remembering. "Mason was our oldest and it never seemed fair that we had to practice on him because we had no idea what we were doing. Unfortunately someone has to be first. John and I always joked that he was our prototype."

Annie laughed. "At least Charlie and Sarah have each other and eventually a therapy buddy when they grow up and complain that we did it all wrong. At least me. Mason is so good with them."

It was clearer every day how much he loved his children, as if he'd been waiting a very long time to be a father. Unlike Dwayne, the douche who'd called her precious babies another man's brats. When she'd told Mason that, she'd been afraid he'd chase down the jerk and pop him like the douchebag he was. The thought of that was pretty hot.

"Mason told me about your boyfriend abandoning you," Flo said.

"Ex-boyfriend." Annie was going to add "mind reader" to this woman's list of superpowers. "I couldn't have been more wrong about him. I won't make a mistake like that again."

"Not everyone walks out."

"Couldn't prove that by me." Annie was afraid the other woman could look into her soul and see the feelings she was trying to hide. Then the meaning of her words sank in. "I wasn't talking about you. I must have sounded completely ungrateful. I'm not sure how I would have coped if not for Mason and you guys, his family."

"We're your family, too."

"I appreciate you saying that." But she wouldn't let herself count on it. The *stepfather* had always said she and Jessica wouldn't have been so much trouble if they'd been his blood. The message had been received loud and clear. Mason's family were helping, but only because of the blood connection to the babies. Why else would they bother?

"I mean it, Annie. Of course having trust is hard." Flo hesitated then added, "You don't have any reason to believe someone who just tells you he loves you. Believe someone who shows you he does."

She was right about trust. Annie's biological father physically left. The stepfather emotionally dumped her. Then she made the mistake of letting her guard down with Dwayne. Three strikes and you're out.

Annie didn't believe in love anymore. Disillusionment hurt and the longer she stayed here in this house with Mason, the more she could get sucked into believing. As soon as she could manage on her own, she was going back to her place.

Mason sat in the rocker that was older than he was and held Sarah in his arms. Annie was next to him in the glider chair, her bad leg elevated on the ottoman and Charlie nestled to her chest. It was late and everyone else in the house was asleep. To keep it that way, they were tandem rocking the twins.

He glanced sideways and thought how beautiful she looked with a baby in her arms. She and the twins had been here for two weeks and it was the best two weeks he'd had in a very long time. Charlie whimpered restlessly and she softly shushed, settling him down.

Annie met his gaze and frowned. "What?" she whispered.

"Nothing." He studied Sarah and knew now that she was sufficiently asleep to handle a quiet conversation.

Annie kept staring. "You have kind of a dweeby look on your face. Why?"

"It's the same look I always have. Guess I'm just a dweeb."

"No." She shook her head.

"So you don't think I'm a dweeb?"

"I didn't say that. Your expression is just dweebier than normal." She rubbed a hand over Charlie's back. "What are you thinking about? It's making you look weird."

He hesitated. "I feel silly telling you."

"Now I have to know." There was a teasing note in her voice.

"You'll mock me."

"Probably. Suck it up, Doc. You're a grown man. A soldier. I can't believe you haven't developed a thicker skin."

Maybe a diversionary tactic would distract her. "Have you?"

"I had to." She laughed but there was no humor in the sound. "For survival. So let me help you exercise those muscles. What were you thinking to put that dopey expression on your face?"

"Well, I should start by saying that I'm sorry you broke your leg." *But not for helping you shower.* It was on his highlight reel of awesome memories, but he didn't think she'd want to know that.

"Not as sorry as I am. But how is that silly?"

"Because I'm not sorry about being under the same roof with you. And my children," he added. "So I can get to know them better. Like now."

"You're rocking Sarah to sleep," she pointed out. "How is that getting to know her?"

"I'm doing it in the rocking chair that my father bought for my mother when she was pregnant with me." It had been out in the garage and brought in because sometimes both babies needed rocking.

"So it's an antique," she teased.

"I'm not going to let you spoil this for me." He smiled at her. "I'm learning about her sleep patterns. And Charlie's. Figuring out what it takes to soothe them when they're upset. Their personalities. I get to just be around. Before it was like visiting hours at the hospital and now— It's not."

"You'd probably rather have them on their own. Without me."

"No," he assured her. "You're their mom. The engine that drives everything. The center of their world."

"And you really don't mind that your world is turned upside down because I broke my leg and the three of us had to move in?"

"Just the opposite. I love what I do for a living. I love

being a doctor and helping people, but it doesn't compare to being a father and spending as much time as possible with my children. Like I said, I'm glad you're here. In fact, I'd have to say, for maybe the first time in my life, I'm content."

He wasn't pulling all-nighters for grades to get him into med school or stressing about the money to go. It wasn't about looking at the calendar to gauge his wife's ovulation date or trying to get pregnant. There was no agenda except to just be. And while he was just being, he could feel Annie's gaze on him.

"What?" he asked.

"You're right. What you were thinking about was dopey. And sweet," she added.

"Haven't you ever experienced contentment?"

"It's hard to feel something you don't believe in. If contentment exists, it's just the bubble of calm between crises."

His mother had mentioned to him that she'd talked with Annie about her absentee parents and Dwayne the Douche. It explained her tendency toward cynicism, but he had the feeling there was more. He saw a lot of people in the emergency room and often they withheld information, reluctant to admit some aspect of their lifestyle might be contributing to whatever condition needed medical intervention. He couldn't help without all the facts and had learned to spot the signs. Annie was holding out, but maybe he could change that.

"Do you want to talk about what happened to you, besides a self-centered boyfriend who left you in the lurch?"

"Life happened," she said. "Dwayne was just the cherry on top of a bad-luck sundae."

"Tell me about it." Sarah was deadweight in his arms,

sound asleep. But if he put her in the crib, this moment of quiet reflection would disappear and he didn't want it to.

"My mother got pregnant in her senior year of high school and was pressured to marry the boy she slept with. They were on their own and hardly more than kids themselves. Barely two years later, I was on the way. He couldn't handle the responsibility of two kids and took off."

That explained why Dwayne's desertion had hit a supersensitive nerve. "You mentioned a stepfather."

"Right." Bitterness was thick in her voice. "He's the man my mother married, but calling him a father is really stretching the definition of the word."

"What happened?" It surprised him a little when she answered because she was quiet for so long.

"You should probably know that I have dyslexia. There could be a hereditary component."

"Okay."

"If either of the twins has trouble reading, we need to look into getting them help as soon as possible."

"That's good to know." The tension and snap in her tone told him diagnosis and help had been a problem for her. "What happened to you, Annie?"

She wrapped Charlie a little more securely in her arms and softly kissed his forehead. "In elementary school, they didn't pick it up with me for a couple of years. Most of the kids were reading and comprehending in first and second grade. They were off and running."

"But not you."

"No. They tested us and arranged everyone accordingly, giving each group a color. It was supposed to be discreet, but everyone knew who was high, middle and low. I got help through the school district's resource program but needed more than they could give. My teacher suggested private reading and speech therapy, but my mother's husband said it was a waste of money. That I was just stupid."

"Oh, Annie—" A fierce, protective feeling welled up inside him followed closely by an even fiercer anger. And he didn't know how to vent it. It wasn't like he could fly to Florida and punch the guy's lights out for being an insensitive moron. But he was afraid to say anything, partly because he was so ticked off at the jerk. Partly because he sensed she wasn't finished yet.

"He used to put me down every chance he got. Called me dumb. Idiot. Retarded. Whatever insult popped into his tiny little mind."

"Where was your mom?"

"Right there when he did it. Too timid to say anything that would make him walk out and leave her alone with my sister and me."

"So *you* were all alone." It took a lot of effort to keep his voice neutral, to not let her see how outraged he was on her behalf.

"No. I had Jessica."

"She was just a kid herself," he said.

"Which makes her actions even more special." She looked at him over Charlie's head. "When he'd start in on me for no reason, she would run interference. And sometimes it would distract him and she'd take the brunt of whatever verbal abuse he was handing out."

"Good for her." He remembered a tough self-awareness about the woman he'd spent one night with. And this was where it had come from.

"He liked to ground us for any small thing, but never together because we had fun."

"Piece of work—" Mason said under his breath.

"And at school. There were bullies who used to make fun of me. But not when my sister was around and she made it a point to be around as much as she could. She was my hero." Annie sighed and it was an achingly sad and profoundly lonely sound. "I miss her so much. She would have been a good mom."

"Her protective instincts were extraordinarily strong even then," he agreed. "Oh, Annie, I wish you hadn't had to go through that. No child should."

"What doesn't kill you makes you stronger, right? And I was convinced reading would kill me. For sure it was a challenge and I hated it. But art—" The dislike in her voice turned to reverence. "There's no right or wrong way to do it. It's about the artist's interpretation. I had fantastic teachers who took me under their wings and gave me the best advice I ever got."

"Which was?"

"Study what you love. I did that and found a career."

"And you're good at it," he said.

"I'm not looking for pity. I just thought you should know because we'll be co-parenting. And—" She caught her bottom lip between her teeth.

"What? You can tell me anything." And he hoped she would.

"You might have noticed that sometimes I have a chip on my shoulder. It's my hard outer shell, my bulletproof vest against humiliation."

"In the army I saw men and women ripped apart even with body armor. It can't protect against everything. Children can be cruel, but most grow out of it to become better human beings. You might want to cut people slack sometimes. No one is perfect."

"Says the guy with the perfect childhood. Raised by the perfect parents, with a father who bought his wife a rocking chair when she was pregnant."

"It was good," he admitted. "And I wouldn't change a

thing. It's the way I want Charlie and Sarah to grow up. But there's no such thing as perfect. You have to learn to roll with the punches."

She lifted Charlie from her shoulder and settled him on his back in her lap. He was getting so big he barely fit. Then she rotated her arm to ease the stiffness. "I'm not looking for perfect. I just learned to take things one mess at a time and always have a plan B."

Mason had studied anatomy, physiology; he knew how to heal bodies. But wounded souls were not his specialty. He wanted to take away her pain, and all the bad stuff in her past, and had no clue how to do that. For a man whose whole life was about fixing people, that was a tough reality.

All he could do was show up so she would know he wasn't going anywhere. They shared the same goal: loving these children. That would never change and it was safe for him.

Romantic love was different—mercurial—even when you thought you had all the bases covered. It was humbling and painful and something he was determined to never do again.

He wanted Annie. No question about that, but that was just anatomy and physiology. He wouldn't let it become more. Because of the children. And speaking of the twins...

"Tomorrow you and I are going to go house hunting," he said.

Chapter Six

The next morning when Annie walked into the kitchen Mason was there, leaning against the counter by the sink with a cup of coffee in his hand. Every time she saw him it was like being starstruck all over again, making her breath catch and her heart pound. Today was no exception. Most women would be excited about the reaction, but Annie wasn't most women.

Last night she hadn't challenged him about the house hunting remark because they were trying to settle the twins. Now she had questions. "About a house…" she said.

"I'm going out with a Realtor today and I'd like you to come along. If you don't have anything pressing at work," he added.

"No, I'm caught up. My boss has all my ideas and sketches related to the account we're going after, but…" She leaned on her crutches and stared at him. She had another question. "What about the twins?"

"My mom is working half a day and will be home soon to watch them."

Annie's first reaction was no way. She hadn't been

alone with him since the drive to the emergency room when she broke her leg. Although, technically, they had been alone that first night in this house when he'd helped her shower. She'd felt the burn ever since and not from hot water. It was all about the hotness of this man. So pretty to look at, which distracted her from the fact that he could not possibly be as good as he seemed. No man was.

"Annie, please say something." He set his mug on the counter.

"You can't want me to go. With these crutches, I'll just slow you down."

"Not that much. You're getting around pretty well now. Are you having any pain?"

"You sound like a doctor."

"Because I am." He smiled. "So, are you? In any pain, I mean."

"No. But my leg is itching like crazy."

"I know it's uncomfortable. Believe it or not, that's a good sign," he said. "On the bright side, getting out and doing something will distract you."

"Why?"

"You'll be focused on something else and not thinking about how much you want to find something that will fit down that cast and scratch the itch."

She couldn't help smiling because he was right about wanting desperately to do just that. But that wasn't what she'd asked. "I meant why do you want me to go along?"

"Since the twins will be with me half the time, I'd really like your input. A mother's perspective on their potential environment. I've been working with a real-estate agent and he's lined up some houses based on the criteria I gave him." Mason folded his arms over his chest. "I could really use another point of view, especially about safety concerns, kid-friendly floor plans. Another pair of eyes to pick up something I might not see or think about."

"You had a house before you deployed. Why did you sell it?" She wouldn't have blurted that out except he'd backed her into a corner. But when the happy look on his face faded to dark and his eyes turned intense, she felt guilty enough to let it go. "If you really want me there, I'll go. But you need to let me know if I'm holding you back. You don't have a lot of time, what with work, and I don't want to slow you down."

"Promise." With his index finger he made an X over his heart. "I'd really like to get this done. Find a place of my own. You know what they say about a guy in his thirties who lives with his mother."

She laughed. "Yeah. People are starting to talk. 'There's something odd about Dr. Blackburne. He still lives at home.'"

"I know, right?" One corner of his mouth curved up and just like that the darkness was gone. "And I think the twins need their own space. Sometimes we just need to let them cry and it's hard to do that here because we don't want them disturbing anyone else."

"Good point. Okay. I need to change." She glanced down at her old sweatpants, legs cut off to accommodate the cast. "If potential neighbors see a bag lady trailing you, no one will sell you an outhouse."

"Yeah." But something shifted in his expression when his gaze skimmed her legs, and humor was replaced by what looked a lot like hunger. He turned away and reached into the sink. "While you do that, I'll wash bottles and get them ready so Mom won't have to deal with it when she comes home."

Annie hobbled out of the room and prayed she wasn't making a big mistake going with him. However, she'd given her word and wouldn't back out. Besides, she had bigger problems. Like what to wear. Fortunately the October weather was still warm, at least during the day. Bermuda shorts would work. She chose white ones and a T-shirt with lime-green horizontal stripes and three-quarter-length sleeves.

Before going in the bathroom, she peeked at the babies in the crib and was glad they were still sleeping soundly. She was getting pretty good at balancing on one leg and braced her midsection against the sink while pulling her hair back into a ponytail. After taking more care with her makeup than normal, she told herself that it had everything to do with making a good impression on a potential neighborhood and nothing to do with impressing Mason. And she almost believed the lie.

Flo came home just as Annie was ready, so it appeared the universe was aligning for her to go with him.

A short time later they'd met the agent, George Watters, and were now pulling up in front of a house. "Note the beautifully maintained landscape," he said. "Brick walkway. Covered front porch. Four bedrooms, two-and-a-half baths. I'm sorry, Annie, but this is a two-story home."

"That's not a problem," Mason said before she could comment. "We'll check out the first floor and see if it's even necessary to look upstairs."

After everyone exited the SUV and went up the walkway, George extracted a key from the lockbox and let them inside. Using the crutches, Annie swung herself over the threshold and looked around. It was an older home with low ceilings and needed a fresh coat of paint. There was an eat-in kitchen, but not a lot of counter space. Still, the family room was adjacent, so being able to keep an eye on the twins while fixing dinner was a plus.

Annie couldn't tell what Mason thought. She wasn't

blown away, but he was the one buying it. "What do you think?"

He was staring out the sliding-glass door into the back-yard. Turning, he said, "I was hoping for a little more space for the twins to play."

"No problem," George said. "This is just the first one. I've got more for you and your wife to look at."

"We're not married," Annie said.

"I should know better than to assume." George was silver-haired, in his mid to late fifties, and looked apologetic.

"No problem. It was an honest mistake." Mason didn't elaborate.

That was for the best, Annie thought. The phrase "it's complicated" was tossed around a lot, but with her and Mason and the twins, it really *was* complicated. The situation would be a challenge to clarify in twenty-five words or less.

"So let's go look at option number two," the agent suggested.

They piled back in the SUV and George drove them to another property that wasn't far from the hospital. The front yard was basic but well cared for and there was a front porch. For some reason Annie was drawn to covered front porches, picturing it with a couple of chairs for sitting outside in the evening. Chatting with neighbors. Watching kids play until it was time to go inside to get ready for bed. The vivid fantasy made her wistful.

George unlocked the door and let them in. The walls were painted a neutral shade of beige with contrasting white doors and trim. Mason checked out the rear yard and nodded approvingly. The kitchen had granite countertops, an island and lots of cupboards.

"Thoughts?" Mason said.

"It's nice. Let me take another look." She walked, or rather, hobbled, the complete bottom floor again and stopped by the stairs. "It has possibilities."

"Okay. Let's look upstairs."

"I can't get up there, but you go ahead," she urged Mason. "I'll wait here."

"I want your opinion on the entire house." He instructed her to rest the crutches against the railing, then scooped her up and carried her to the second floor.

Annie protested but slid her arms around his neck. "For a doctor you're not too bright. Your back will not thank you for this."

"I'm showing off." He grinned. "And you don't weigh much."

That made her heart happy and way too soon the top floor was visible. There was an open loft that looked down on the entryway. Mason walked her through three bedrooms and then the master. One very nice feature was a balcony overlooking the backyard, but they both thought the rooms were on the small side. Annie made him look in the closet and she felt it left a lot to be desired.

"But that might not matter to you," she said.

Unless a woman moved in with him. The thought was vaguely unappealing. It shouldn't be, and the fact that it was bothered her more than a little. Then it occurred to her that another woman would be around her children. And she had no right to say anything about who he became involved with. Well, shoot.

"I wouldn't have noticed that," Mason said. "That's why I wanted you to come with me. Still, there are a lot of positive things here. We'll make a list of pros and cons."

"Okay."

Annie found herself wishing the trip back down those stairs wouldn't end too soon. It gave her the opportunity to hold him, to feel her body close to his. She wasn't the one exerting herself but was a little breathless anyway. It didn't mean anything, she told herself. Just that while her leg might be broken, her female parts were working just fine.

At the bottom of the stairs Mason set her down and she missed the warmth of him. He handed her the crutches and looked up to where they'd just been.

"I was just thinking about the twins. When they start crawling. They'll go right for the stairs."

George joined them. "You can get gates for the bottom and the top. Until they're old enough to go up and down by themselves."

"I suppose." But Mason didn't look sure about that.

So they got back in the SUV and went to two more houses. Both were adequate but nothing to get excited about.

"I've got one more," George said. "It just came on the market. And it's one story."

When they stopped at the curb Annie zeroed in on the covered porch. Check, she thought. The yard was landscaped with neatly trimmed bushes and flowers. Inside was a traditional floor plan: living and dining rooms separated by a marble-tiled entryway. There was no furniture and George explained that because of a job transfer, the family had to leave quickly. That meant they'd probably be willing to make a deal and escrow could move fast. But first things first. They needed to look at the whole house.

The kitchen was gorgeous—beautiful granite, white cupboards—and she didn't even care about toddler handprints. There was a copper rack for pots and pans hanging over the island.

The rest of the house had spacious bedrooms and big closets. Mason heartily approved of the backyard and there was a casita. She looked inside and couldn't help thinking what a great home office it could be. But it wouldn't be her home or her office. Or her man. He was the twins' father. That was all.

"What do you think?" Mason asked.

Without hesitation she said, "I love everything about this house."

He smiled at her. "Me, too. I'm going to make an offer."

While he talked details with the Realtor, Annie browsed the rooms again. With every hobbling step she took, the longing for a traditional family grew. What she wouldn't give for the twins to have a father and mother. Correction, they had that. What she yearned for was all of them together in this house, a family unit, a happy home with kids. And marriage. Traditional all the way.

She hated being right about making a mistake coming with Mason to look at houses. Now there was a happy picture in her head, but reality never lived up to the image. If she'd never seen this place, she'd never have known what she was going to miss.

And she was going to miss being a family and living in this house.

Once a month the Blackburne family had dinner together. Attendance was mandatory unless you were bleeding, on fire, working or deployed to a foreign country. This ritual was one of the things Mason had missed most when he was gone. Today the family gathering had grown by two with the twins. Three counting Annie. She was the mother of his children and a part of them now.

Mason put a big blanket on the floor in the family room, set out toys in the center of it, then settled the twins on their backs.

Annie was sitting on the large sofa that separated the

kitchen and family rooms. She was sporting a brand-new, hot-pink walking cast since her recent follow-up orthopedic appointment. After a month the bone was healing nicely, but the doc didn't want her to put weight on it for another two weeks. A cautious approach of which Mason highly approved. For any patient, but especially for Annie.

She met his gaze and smiled. "They're not going to stay put on that blanket."

"I know." They'd grown so much in the last two months, rolling all over and getting up on all fours to rock back and forth, the prelude to crawling. That milestone wasn't very far off.

"As you well know, those toys are far less interesting than electrical cords and everything breakable."

"And I couldn't be prouder," he said. "They're curious. Exploring their environment is exactly what they're supposed to do at this age."

His dad took the roast outside to barbecue and his mom walked over to stand behind the couch, wiping her hands on a dish towel. "Gabriel and Dominic aren't used to babies on the floor. Charlie and Sarah aren't like Lulu, who can get out of the way. Will they be okay?"

"My brothers or the twins?"

Flo laughed. "I was talking about the babies. We have to make sure everyone watches their step."

"Don't worry," Annie said. "I'm on it. I may not be able to move very fast, but I can direct traffic and, if all else fails, I've got my crutches. To make a point."

"Funny," Mason said and she smiled. He really liked her smile.

"It's too bad Kelsey had to work." His mom leaned a hip on the back of the sofa. "You're a doctor. You couldn't pull some strings to get her off?"

"Two things, Ma. I haven't been there very long, so

zero influence. And I'm not in charge of the nurses' scheduling." He grabbed up Charlie, who'd already rolled off the blanket onto his stomach and had his eye on something across the room. "Hey, bud, where do you think you're going?"

When the doorbell rang, Lulu started barking and rushed to greet whoever was there, waiting patiently for someone taller and with opposable thumbs to open the door.

Mason put a squirming Charlie back on the blanket and looked at Annie. "It's about to get wild. Brace yourself."

"It occurs to me that for the last five months I've lived in a constant state of being braced."

And it looked good on her. Normally her hair was pulled up in a ponytail, out of her way when she was busy with babies. Today it was down and fell past her shoulders, shiny and blond. For some reason the silky strands framing her face made her hazel eyes look more green. Or it might be the pink lip gloss. She was a woman who would turn men's heads and his brothers were both single. The thought had him bracing—for what he wasn't sure.

The two men walked into the room and bro-hugged Mason. They all had blue eyes and brown hair—clones, his mother always said about the family resemblance. Gabe and Dom knew about Annie and the twins but this was the first time they'd met.

Flo smiled at her sons. "I have to finish getting the rest of dinner ready. Mason, you handle introductions."

"Okay." He looked at his brothers. "This is Annie, the twins' mother."

The taller of the two moved closer and shook her hand. "I'm Gabriel. Sorry about your leg. Nice to meet you."

"Same here." She looked ruefully at the cast. "My fault for not watching where I was going."

"I'm Dominic." He was the youngest of the boys and had a thin scar on his chin. The details were never clear but it had something to do with a girl.

"Nice to meet you." She looked past Mason. "And those two little troublemakers are your niece and nephew, color coded. Sarah's in pink and—"

"Charlie's the one in blue who is checking out the movie collection." Mason moved quickly to grab him up before the stack of plastic DVD containers toppled on him. "He's moving faster all the time."

"And Sarah is right behind." Annie indicated the little girl who was scooting in the same direction as her brother. "She's ready to follow into whatever trouble he leads her."

"Cute kids," Dom said. "They look like Annie."

"Subtle, bro." Mason held his son and the curious little boy checked out the neckline of his T-shirt then explored his nose and ear.

"So you're a graphic artist," Gabe said to Annie.

"Yes."

Mason hadn't mentioned anything about her job. "How did you know that?"

"Her firm did a branding campaign for Make Me a Match. It was well-done. Smart. Clever. Visual."

"Thanks." The dog trotted over to Annie and she patted the seat beside her. Lulu didn't have to be asked twice and jumped up for a belly rub. "My friend Carla works for you. We met while I was involved in the project."

"Actually she's my aunt's personal assistant. And I'm only working there temporarily."

"So she said. I understand the business is still not where you'd like, financially speaking," Annie commented.

"True." His mouth pulled tight. "Aunt Lil is more focused on idealistic notions of relationships than numbers."

Their mother walked over to join the conversation and

clearly she'd been listening in. "My sister is a romantic and always has been. Did you know she fixed up your father and me?"

The three brothers stared at each other with equally blank expressions. Mason said, "That's news to me."

"Did she charge you for her services?" Gabe asked wryly.

"Of course she didn't."

Lulu barked once and jumped off the couch then trotted over to Sarah, who was reaching for the DVDs her brother had just looked over. Mason put Charlie back on the blanket and picked up his daughter.

"Her romanticism is the problem," Gabe continued. "Aunt Lil is in love with love and wants to give it away for free. It's a business and by definition the purpose of its existence is to provide a service for which customers are prepared to pay. In other words, make money."

Flo looked at Annie. "Lillian is a widow. She and Phil were deeply in love until the day he died. They never had children but she always says they were rich in so many ways because they had each other. She wants everyone to have what she did with her husband."

"They were lucky." Mason wasn't interested in what his aunt was selling. "Not everyone is."

"Is that the voice of experience?" Annie asked.

"Yes. I was married and the magic didn't last."

Annie had asked him why he'd sold his house before he deployed. He could have kept it, shut things down until he returned. But it held nothing but bad memories—loss, pain and a marriage imploding with no way to fix it.

Lulu sat on the baby blanket and Charlie touched her back. The dog was extraordinarily patient with the babies and was loving, even protective. While Mason cuddled

Sarah close, he caught Annie considering him, surprise in her eyes.

Then she turned to Gabe. "How do you match people up?"

"Clients fill out a profile, with a picture, then define their likes and dislikes. An algorithm picks up key words to narrow down potentially compatible people. Then we have that group fill out a more detailed questionnaire."

"What kind of questions?" Dom asked. He looked uncharacteristically interested.

Gabe thought for a moment. "Things like 'If you could share dinner with anyone in the world, who would it be?' Or 'If you could be a character in a movie, which one would you choose?' A very revealing one is 'Tattoo—for or against?'"

"Let's try it," his mother suggested. She looked at Annie and Mason. "You take the quiz."

Annie looked a little startled. "I don't know about Mason, but I'm not looking for a match."

"I know. It's just for fun," Flo said. "You're both single. Gabriel, give them a question."

"Okay." He sat on the couch. "How about which character in a movie. You first, Annie."

"Wow. No pressure." She blew out a breath. "Okay. I'd want to be Wonder Woman."

"You're already a superhero," his mom said.

"How sweet. Thanks, Flo."

"I mean it. Twins? That says it all."

"Actually it's not the superpowers I want," Annie clarified. "But that golden lasso would come in pretty handy. A way to know someone is telling the truth."

"Okay. Good answer," Dom said. "Mason, you're probably going to say Superman."

"No." He'd had time to think. "Sherlock Holmes."

"Because the supersleuth is so in touch with his feelings?" Gabe teased.

"No. He notices little things and figures out who's guilty. I can relate to that. I do a lot of mystery-solving in the ER because people don't always give me all the facts. Their symptoms are very general and vague. So I have to read between the lines to help them. It's my job to figure out what's wrong."

"Good answers, both of you," Gabe said. "But I'm not sure they would intersect for a match."

"Okay, next question," his mother said. "I like the tattoo one. How do you feel about them?"

"Not a fan. Don't have one and no plans to get one," Mason answered.

"Okay. The doctor doesn't like needles," Dominic teased.

"But you were in the army," Annie said.

"A tattoo is not a prerequisite for joining," he answered.

"Annie? What about you?" his mother asked.

She squirmed then sighed. "I have one. And I love it."

Mason looked at her, the skin he could see, and couldn't find her ink. His curiosity cranked up by a lot to know what it was and—more important—where. Discovering the location would involve taking clothes off and his body reacted enthusiastically to that thought.

"Strike two." Gabriel shook his head. "Last one. Who would you want to have dinner with?"

"That's easy," Annie said. "Eunice Golden."

"Who?" they all said at the same time.

"I was an art major. She's a painter and a pioneer in her field, focusing on nude male bodies in her earlier work."

Mason noted that the rest of his family looked as clueless and surprised as he felt. And now it was his turn. "I'd like to have dinner with the Surgeon General of the United States Army."

Gabe gave him a pitying look. "Probably no overlap there."

"Even though that person is a woman, appointed for the next couple years?"

"Too subtle." Gabriel shrugged. "If you were clients of Make Me a Match, you would not be paired off."

"Then it's a good thing neither one of us is looking to do that," Annie said.

"Oh, pooh," his mother said. "A few questions on a quiz isn't everything."

Mason had mixed feelings. On the surface they might not look compatible, but he agreed with his mom that a quiz didn't come with a guarantee of success. Everything in his first marriage had looked ideal, but together he and his wife were a disaster. Still, a quiz was stupid. Right? He agreed with Annie about that. He wasn't looking for a match any more than she was. He'd never failed a test in his life. Surely that's what was bothering him now.

Chapter Seven

Her hormones didn't take that matchmaking quiz but
you wouldn't know it by the way they were stirred up.

Annie hadn't been able to stop thinking about those
questions, through dinner and the rest of the evening. Now
it was quiet in the house. Mason's brothers had gone and
everyone else was in bed. The two of them were standing side by side, just putting the twins down. She had the
crutches under her arms but didn't put much weight on
them. Their arms brushed and she felt the contact all the
way to her toes.

According to their answers to those questions, they
weren't compatible, but her body wasn't paying any attention. Still, she had another question for Mason. She
hadn't wanted to interrogate him in front of his family,
but no one else was here now.

"Why didn't you tell me you were married?"

He glanced at the babies, who were drowsy but not
sound asleep yet, and put a shushing finger to his lips.
He angled his head toward the connecting bathroom and
indicated she should follow him. Not wanting to disturb

the twins, she limped after him. When he flipped the switch on the wall in his room, a nightstand lamp came on. There was a king-size bed with a brass headboard and an oak dresser with matching armoire.

Mason met her gaze. "I wasn't keeping it a secret. If I was still married, I'd have said something. But I'm not. The fact that I was married just never came up and it didn't cross my mind to mention that I'm divorced."

Logically that was true, but somehow it felt very relevant to Annie that she didn't know he'd been legally committed to a woman at one time. He'd taken that step because he'd been in love. It should simply be a fact from his past, just information, but she was having a reaction to this fact and it wasn't positive. She wasn't proud of it, but this feeling had a good many characteristics of jealousy.

And then she really looked into his eyes and saw the sadness. Facts were one thing; emotions were something else.

"Do you want to talk about it?" she asked.

He laughed but there was no humor in the sound. "You know those were the first words your sister said to me."

"Oh?"

He nodded. "My divorce was just final and I went to the bar. She was already there and came over, sat down on the stool next to me."

"She must have thought you looked sad. Like you do now." She moved closer to where he stood at the foot of the bed. Their bodies didn't touch but she could feel the warmth of his. "Did you tell her what was going on?"

"Only that my divorce became final that day but not why it happened in the first place. She heard the *D* word and suggested that there was a rebound activity guaranteed to take my mind off it."

Annie winced. It was hard to hear about her sister's

behavior. Jess was always there for her and she'd never forget it. "She wasn't a bad person."

"I know. That night we both needed a way to forget the stuff that was eating away at us."

"What were you trying to block out?" she asked.

"Failure. On so many levels." He sighed. "I fell in love with Christy and that was obviously not a success. I was in town to see my family, on leave from the army, when I met her at Patrick's Place, formerly The Pub. That's where I ran into your sister." He smiled. "She was beautiful and funny."

Annie wanted to hear about the woman he'd loved. "So, on the day your divorce was final you went back to the scene of the crime, so to speak."

"Yeah. I guess closure was on my mind. Coming full circle. A place to reflect on what went wrong." He smiled sadly. "The night Christy and I met, we couldn't stop talking. We were kicked out at closing time and sat on a bench outside for hours. Just talking."

"About what?" Annie asked.

"About what we wanted. Mostly that we both very much wanted to have children." He smiled at her. "I love kids. I'm like my mom that way. In fact, I thought about being a pediatrician for a while."

"Why didn't you?"

"I liked the adrenaline rush of emergency medicine."

"So what happened? With Christy, I mean."

"We had a long-distance relationship, but it worked, and then I proposed. We bought a house here in Huntington Hills. After all, I wouldn't be in the army forever and this town is where we wanted to settle and raise kids. We had a church wedding with both families there. She even got pregnant on our honeymoon. Everything was perfect."

"Magic," she said quietly.

That soul-deep sadness turned his eyes as hard as blue diamonds. "Until it wasn't."

"She lost the baby." Annie was just guessing.

He met her gaze and nodded. "We both took it hard, but she was really sucker punched. After all, she'd had a life inside her. And then it was gone. The doctor said we could try again right away, but I wanted to wait. She insisted we go for it and I gave in to make her happy."

Annie knew what he was going to say and just waited for him to put it into words.

"That time she made it almost through the first trimester before the miscarriage."

"Oh, Mason—" She put a hand over her mouth. "I can't even begin to imagine how hard that was for you both."

"And I don't have the words to explain the devastation we felt. The first time we believed—hoped—it was a fluke. Just one of those things. And the doctor assured us that it happens and no one can explain why. No reason we couldn't have more babies without any problems at all. Other couples did all the time."

"But not you." If this had a happy ending, the two of them wouldn't be standing there right now.

"The second miscarriage meant there was a pattern. Made us doubt we could have what we wanted most. Christy wanted to try again, right away, but this time I held firm on waiting." He dragged his fingers through his hair. "When a body goes through trauma like that, conventional wisdom suggests a sufficient amount of time to rest and rejuvenate." He looked lost in memories that were bad and it seemed as if he was going to stay there, but he finally went on. "She was angry. We both knew there was an overseas deployment in my future and she wanted a baby before that. We were drifting apart emotionally and physically. I suggested date nights, brought her flowers, tried to get back the dream we'd both wanted when we first met."

"And?"

"She was closed off. Until one night she came to me and was so much like the woman she'd been. I thought we were finding our way back. We had sex. She didn't mention that she had stopped birth control."

"She got pregnant?"

"Yes." A muscle in his cheek jerked and his eyes flashed with anger. "And she lost that baby, too."

"I'm so sorry, Mason."

He sighed. "That's when she gave up on us. I wanted to go to counseling, try to make things work. There were other ways to have the family we wanted. Surely we could be like my aunt Lillian and uncle Phil. But I couldn't fix what was wrong all by myself. No matter how much I wanted to."

"That's so sad."

"Yeah, sad. A small word for what I felt. I didn't just lose my children, I lost my wife. My family. I couldn't save anything. And I hated that house full of sad reminders."

"That's why you sold it before you were deployed," Annie said.

He nodded. "Most guys who shipped out left behind a wife and their kids. They didn't want to go, but sacrificed that time with loved ones in service to their country. But I couldn't wait to get out of here. I was glad to go."

"To leave the bad stuff behind."

"Yes. And to do some good. I couldn't help Christy, but I saved lives. To the best of my ability I stabilized the wounded, made sure soldiers who experienced traumatic injuries didn't lose an arm or leg. They thanked me for healing them, but it was just the opposite. They healed me." He met her gaze. "Then I got your email."

"About the babies possibly being yours."

He nodded. "I didn't know what to feel. So many times before I'd expected and hoped to have children. I didn't want to go all in again and get kicked in the teeth. Or was it just a cruel hoax? A miracle? A scam?"

"You're not the only one who thought that," she said wryly.

"I could have sent you a DNA sample, but I wanted to meet you—" he glanced past her, toward the room where the two babies slept side by side in a crib "—and the twins before doing it. Just being here made me feel more in control." He shrugged and there was a sheepish expression on his face. "Stupid, really. I know better than anyone control is an illusion. Because if it was up to me, those pregnancies would have resulted in healthy babies not miscarriages."

"And you might still be married," she said.

"I'm not so sure about that. I began to wonder if we just needed to believe we were in love because of wanting children so much. Thanks to science there are more options to have a family and I tried to talk to her about that or adoption, but she couldn't stand that everything wasn't normal, neat and tidy. Perfect. If she couldn't have that, she didn't want anything. Including me. By my definition, that isn't love."

It was such a devastating story of life dumping on him and love lost. And Mason looked so incredibly sad at the memories of the children who would never be. Annie couldn't help herself. She had to touch him, offer comfort. She moved one step closer and rested her crutches against the bed then put her arms around him.

"I'm so sorry you went through that, Mason."

He held completely still when her body pressed against his and didn't react for several moments. Annie was afraid that she'd somehow made things worse and started to step away.

"No."

She looked up and saw the conflict in his eyes just before he pulled her against him and lowered his mouth to hers. That achingly sweet touch set off fireworks inside her. It felt as if she'd been waiting for this since the moment she'd opened her door and seen him standing there in military camouflage, looking as exhausted as she'd felt.

Annie pressed her body closer but it wasn't enough as heat poured through her and exploded between them. He settled his hands at her waist then slid them down to her butt and squeezed softly before cupping her breasts in his palms. The kiss turned more intense as he brushed his tongue over her lower lip. She opened to him and let him explore, let the fire burn.

He backed up toward the bed and circled her waist with his arm, half carrying her with him. The only sound in the room was their combined breathing and it was several moments before they both heard a baby's whimper.

"It's Charlie." She pulled away and started to reach for the crutches but he stopped her.

"Should I apologize, Annie?"

That would mean he was sorry, and she didn't want him to be. She just wanted him so much.

"Annie?"

The whimper became more insistent and she put the crutches under her arms before turning away. "He's going to wake Sarah. You need to grab him, Mason."

He nodded and hurried into the other room.

She was sorry but only because of how very much she wanted him. Giving him that information wasn't smart.

He didn't believe in love any more than she did. So starting anything wasn't the wisest course of action. It had just happened because they were practically living on top of each other.

She could resist him for just a little bit longer. In a short time the cast would be off and she could go back home. And he would close escrow on the house and move into it. Either way, she wouldn't have to go to bed at night with only a bathroom between them.

Just to prove how spineless she was, Annie wasn't sure whether to be sad or glad about that.

It had been several days since Mason had kissed Annie and his son interrupted them. The kid's timing was bad. And she'd never answered the question about whether or not he should apologize for kissing her, touching her. *Wanting* her.

Now he was in bed, alone and frustrated. It was early and quiet, so the twins were not awake yet. He was, mostly because sleep had been hard to come by ever since that kiss. Might as well get up, he thought. There was a lot of house-buying stuff to do today.

He went in the bathroom and listened for sounds and movement on the other side of the door to the room where Annie slept with the babies. It was still quiet. That was good; she needed her sleep. After a shower and shave, he dressed in jeans and a T-shirt, then went to the kitchen.

His mother was there. More important, she'd made coffee. Moving a little farther into the room, he saw that Annie was there, too, already having a cup.

"Good morning," she said.

His mother was standing by the counter in front of a waffle iron. "Morning, Mason. Did you sleep well?"

"Like a rock," he lied. "Charlie and Sarah were quiet all night. I didn't hear a peep from them."

"I know." Annie sipped her coffee. "If only we could count on that every night."

Flo laughed. "By the time that happens, they'll be teenagers staying out all night."

"It was one time, Mom," he protested. "And I lost the car for a month. Are you ever going to let me forget that?"

"No." She gave him a look before turning back to watch what she was cooking. "And someone got up on the wrong side of the bed this morning. You're crabby."

"For being irritated that you still bring up teenage transgressions?"

"I was joking," she said.

He poured himself a cup of coffee. "Soon I will have my own place and you won't have to put up with me being crabby in the morning."

"Don't remind me."

"It's not like I'm going to the Middle East. The house isn't that far away."

She slid a waffle onto a plate and brought it to the table. "But you'll be gone. Everything's changing around here too fast for my liking."

Annie put butter and syrup on her breakfast and cut off a bite before looking at him. "Your mom and I were just talking about this. My cast is coming off in a couple of days and I'll be going back to my apartment with the babies."

"I'm going to miss all of you terribly," his mother said.

Mason had known this moment would eventually come but hadn't expected the announcement to knock the air out of him. He wasn't ready. "Annie, you need to be careful when the cast comes off and you put weight on the leg. Maybe you should think about staying here a little longer."

"I've already imposed long enough." She looked at his mom, gratitude in her eyes. "As much as I appreciate everything you've done, I don't want to take advantage of your hospitality."

"Please. Use us," Flo pleaded. "Stay as long as you want. We love having you here. It will be too quiet without you. I love those babies so much."

"I know." Annie smiled fondly at the other woman. "And they love you. I appreciate the offer and everything you've done for us more than I can tell you."

Mason was moving out soon and had deliberately put off thinking about being in the new house alone. After being with her and his kids, that was a lonely prospect. Because she'd helped him pick out the house, he couldn't help picturing Annie there. And the reminder that she wouldn't be didn't improve his mood. For that reason, he kept his mouth shut. No point in opening it and proving what his mother had pointed out. That he was crabby. If he did, there would be questions and he wouldn't want to answer them.

Annie was almost finished with her breakfast and sighed with satisfaction. "That was so good."

"If you stay, I'll make them every morning. I'm not above using food as a bribe," his mother said.

"Tempting." Annie grinned.

"At the risk of being pushy, since the twins are still asleep, it might be a good idea to get a shower in before they wake up," Flo said.

"That's not pushy. I was thinking the same thing." She stood and grabbed the crutches resting nearby. "Thanks for breakfast."

"You're very welcome. I'll listen for the babies and bring their bottles to you when they wake up."

"Thanks." She hobbled out of the room and smiled up at him as she passed.

Mason's heart skipped a beat and he resisted the urge to turn and watch her limp away. He'd gotten used to watching her, seeing a smile light up her face. And when he couldn't see it every day, there would be a significant withdrawal period.

His mother poured more coffee into her mug and blew on the top. "You should marry that girl."

It took a couple of moments for the words to sink in. And he still wasn't sure he'd heard her right. "What?"

"You should marry Annie," she said again, as if there was any doubt who "that girl" was.

"I can't believe you just said that. It's outrageous even for you."

"What does that mean? Even for me."

"I mean you can't just say whatever pops into your mind."

"I don't." She cradled her cup between her hands and leaned back against the counter. "That thought came to me when I saw your face. After Annie said she was moving back to her apartment. I didn't say it then. I waited."

"My face? What about it?"

"You looked as if someone just punched you in the gut," his mother said calmly.

"No, I didn't."

"Mason—" It was the dreaded Mom voice. "I know you. And if I'm being honest—"

"When are you not?" he asked wryly.

"It's a gift." She smiled at him. "I've never seen you happier than now—since Annie moved in here with Charlie and Sarah. It gives me such joy to see you this way."

He wanted to tell her she was wrong but he couldn't. It was true. He'd told Annie as much and risked her calling him silly. But from here to marriage was a big leap. "Mom, seriously—"

"I can see how much you like each other." At his look of irritation, she sighed. "I'm old, not dead. And I can see when two people have a connection."

"No one said anything about love. I respect and admire her very much but— And, in case you forgot, we were zero for three on Gabriel's questionnaire."

"I'll deny it if you ever tell him I said this, but that quiz is not helpful. I see the way you and Annie look at each other."

"How is that?"

"Like you want to be alone. There were sparks, Mason, and it's more than respect and admiration."

He didn't want to discuss this. It was crazy. Although there was that really hot kiss. "You're imagining things, Mom."

"I have an imagination, I'll admit. But trust me on this, you and Annie have sparks. Successful marriages have started with less. Including me and your dad."

"You weren't in love when you got married?"

"We were young, wildly attracted to each other. And pregnant with you."

"What?" That was a shock. "I never knew that. You had to get married?"

"We didn't have to. Our parents were supportive. But doing the right thing was important to both of us." She shrugged. "The realization of how much we loved each other came after you were born. We were tired and stressed about making ends meet, but our bond and commitment and love grew stronger every day because of how much we both loved you. Your father was the right man for me and my hormones knew it before my heart did."

The union his parents shared was the bar by which

Mason judged success. He had no idea their deepest commitment to each other had started with him. "Still, Mom—"

"You and Annie have two children together. You're parents and good ones. In spite of Gabriel's dopey quiz, you're compatible. I can see it the way you work together with the babies. If there were any cracks, the strain of caring for them would break them wide open. If anything, you two have grown stronger from the experience."

That statement had the ring of truth to it. "Maybe, but—"

"Please don't go by those completely irrelevant questions. Fortunately your aunt Lillian relies on her instincts about a man and woman when she's matchmaking. Her success rate is pretty high, too." She smiled. "That intuition for pairing up a man and woman runs in the family."

"Even if you're right about Annie and me—"

"I am." She pointed at him. "And you're going to say, why rush things? And I will say, why wait? You care and so does she. Together you can give Charlie and Sarah a stable home, a loving environment. And all of that under one roof."

"This idea is crazy, Mom."

She tapped her lip. "And your paternity petition is still pending with the court. It couldn't hurt to show that you're making a legal commitment to their mother, as well."

"We don't have to be married for me to present a strong case. I have the DNA proof."

"Of course you do. And that was one of those things that just popped into my mind. But this isn't. If you don't get out of your own way and marry her, someone else just might snatch her up, right out from under your nose. That old boyfriend could still be lurking."

"Not after what he called my children." Mason still wanted to clock him for that.

"Maybe not him, but Annie is pretty, smart and funny. Someone is going to sweep her off her feet. It should be you."

When Mason was in medical school, there hadn't been a class on jealousy, but that didn't mean he couldn't diagnose it now. The knot in his gut, elevated blood pressure and the pounding in his temples. All symptoms that confirmed the thought of Annie with another guy was just wrong.

But that didn't answer the question.

What was he going to do about it?

Chapter Eight

Annie sat on the medical exam table at the orthopedic office and watched Dr. Jack Andrews cut through her cast. Mason had driven and was standing by her, but there was something on his mind other than freedom for her leg. She wasn't sure how she knew that but she did.

The doctor shut off the mini-saw and set it aside, then pried apart the cast and cotton-like material beneath that was sticking to her skin. He smiled. "How does the leg feel?"

"Like heaven. But it looks gross. All white and shriveled and different from the other one." She glanced at Mason, not sure she wanted him to see the grossness and not sure why she should care that he did. And it was a waste of energy because he'd already seen.

"Don't worry. That's normal for what you've been through." Dr. Andrews was a colleague of Mason's, young and good-looking, but his opinion on the attractiveness of her leg didn't matter.

"It doesn't look normal." She glanced at Mason again to see if he was grossed out. He didn't look repulsed. He looked like Mason. Strong, steady and incredibly cute Mason.

"Soak the limb in warm water twice a day for the first few days and wash it with mild soap. Use a soft cloth or even gauze. That will help remove the dead skin."

"Does she need to take it easy, Jack?" Just like Mason to ask that.

"As you know, the muscles are atrophied from lack of use. I'm going to prescribe physical therapy for a few weeks so the experts can work on teaching you exercises to strengthen it. In a very short time you'll build the leg up again." He met her gaze, his own serious. "Your balance might be somewhat compromised after weeks of not walking normally. Go slow. Use the crutches at first to see how you do. But it won't be long before you'll forget this ever happened."

"I doubt that." His smile was nice, she thought, but her insides didn't quiver at all from it. Not like when Mason smiled at her.

And the experience hadn't been all bad. She'd gotten to know his family, how wonderful they were. He'd been pretty wonderful, too. The twins were lucky to have him for a father. Was he really determined to stay a bachelor? He was so loving with the babies, it was hard to believe he wouldn't meet a woman who would convince him to try again.

"You've been a perfect patient, Annie."

"And you've been a perfect doctor, Doctor," she said. "No offense but I hope I never have to see you again."

Mason laughed. "She means professionally."

"I got that," the other man said. "The feeling is mutual."

She shook his hand. "Seriously, thank you so much for everything."

"You're welcome."

When they were alone, Mason handed her the sneaker she hadn't used for six weeks.

"Thanks, Mason."

"For?"

"Do I have to pick one thing?" She thought for a moment. "First of all for reminding me to bring my sock and shoe. I'd have forgotten if not for you. It seems like forever since I needed it and I'd have crutched right out of the house without it."

"Happy to help."

"I also want to thank you for going above and beyond the call of duty these last weeks. And for being a good father to the twins."

"I should be thanking you. For making sure I knew about them."

"It was the right thing to do." Her stomach did the quivery thing when he smiled.

"Are you ready to get out of here?"

"So ready." The crutches were braced against the exam table and she grabbed them. "Following doctor's orders. No point in setting myself back. But now I can pick up my babies, not just wait for someone to hand them to me."

"How do you feel about grabbing some lunch before we go home to the kids?"

"Would it be all right with your mom? Does she have to be somewhere?"

"It was her idea." He opened the exam room door.

"In that case, I'm on board."

They walked down the hallway with medical offices on either side, then into the lobby area, where automatic doors opened to the outside. Annie was using the crutches to take part of her weight but felt pretty good moving on her own two feet. No dizziness or pain, just some minor weakness. She felt free, happy, and was looking forward to lunch with Mason.

It was one of those perfect fall days in Southern California and she was enthusiastically on board when he suggested getting sandwiches to eat in the park. There was one a short distance from his new house where they found a picnic table with a roof overhead not far off the cement walkway.

They were sitting side by side, looking at the white gazebo surrounded by yellow-, coral- and pink-flowered bushes. There were towering trees, shrubs, green grass and just a perfect amount of breeze.

"It's so beautiful here." Annie sighed contentedly then took the paper-wrapped turkey sub sandwich and napkin he handed her and immediately unwrapped it.

"Yeah." He set his own lunch on the table and didn't do anything but stare at it.

"I can't wait until Charlie and Sarah are big enough to run around and play on the kids' equipment." She pointed to a bright yellow, blue and red structure with tubes and stairs surrounded by rubberized material for unexpected landings.

"Uh-huh," he answered absently. Definitely distracted about something.

Annie wanted to know what was up with him. Maybe her comment about him being a good father had somehow freaked him out, put pressure on him. With her luck, the bum leg making her dependent on him had made him change his mind about wanting to take responsibility for the twins. Showed him he wasn't cut out for being a dad and he wanted off the hook. She couldn't stand it anymore and had to know.

She put her sandwich down without taking a bite. "Look, just spit it out. Get it over with."

"Spit what out?"

"Whatever it is you're so jumpy about."

"I'm not jumpy." But he didn't sound too sure of that.

"You've been preoccupied since we left the house. The whole time we've been gone you hardly said two words. Except to the doctor. So, just tell me what's going on. I can handle it. I've been alone before."

"What are you talking about?"

"You're responsible enough to not feel comfortable telling me but decent enough to do it to my face. You don't want to be tied down by the twins." The quivery feeling in her stomach became something else that made her want to cry.

He stared at her for several moments then shook his head. "You couldn't be more wrong."

"So I've made a fool of myself and you don't have anything on your mind?"

"No, you're right about that," he confirmed. "I'm actually surprised you know me well enough to recognize that."

"Of course I do." Although she was a little surprised, too. And also really anxious about what was going on in his head. "So, I say again, just get it over with. Please."

"That's what someone says when they think it's going to be something bad."

Damn aviator sunglasses were sexy as all get-out but she couldn't see his eyes. The window to the soul. A clue to what he was feeling. "Because it is bad, right?"

"I didn't think so, but I guess it could be interpreted that way."

"Darn it, Mason. Will you just tell me what we're talking about here?"

"Okay." He blew out a breath. "I was going to ask you to marry me."

Shut the front door! Annie's jaw dropped and she blinked at him for several moments. Unsure what to say, she finally asked, "Why?"

"That should be a simple enough answer but in our case it's complicated." He angled his body toward her. "I don't know where to start."

"So we're not talking love here." Please don't be talking love, she thought. They both had the scars to prove that was a losing proposition.

"Different *L* word. We *like* each other."

"True." And that was so much safer.

"And respect," he said. "I respect you a lot and I'm pretty sure you feel the same about me."

"Definitely." Even when she thought he was going to leave, she gave him credit for doing it in person. "Okay, but we could just go back to the way things were before I broke my leg. I'll move back to my apartment and you can visit any time you want."

He sighed. "I want more. I'll be moving into the house. It just seems like a natural transition to do that together. If I hadn't spent time with you and the kids in the same house, it would have taken me longer to get to this place, but I would have eventually."

"And that is?"

"I don't want to visit my kids. I want to live with them under the same roof, together with their mother. You've said that the apartment is too small and you were going to look for a bigger place." He shrugged. "I just happen to have one. And since the broken leg and living with my folks, you're half out of there anyway. If we just move your stuff to my place, it would be easier. You love the house."

"I do. And your points are all good ones. But we could just live together," she suggested. "Share expenses. Baby-sitting. It's a little unconventional, but this situation is the very definition of that. We don't have to get married to be a family."

He took off his glasses and his eyes were bluer and more intense than ever before. "I want a *traditional* family. For me and for them. With you."

Traditional family. The words struck a chord in Annie's soul, a tune she didn't fully realize had been playing her whole life. She'd never experienced what Mason was offering her. But he had and she'd seen it in action. He knew how to do the family thing. It was as natural to him as breathing. If he was going to abandon her and the twins, he'd have done it already. He wouldn't be offering her a legal commitment.

"Annie?"

"I'm thinking." She met his gaze. "Maybe we should try dating or something first?"

"So you don't want a traditional relationship."

"I didn't say that. Actually, I've wanted that my whole life," she admitted.

"Okay. We could date, but we'll wind up right back here. I feel as if we've been more than dating since we met. And it's been pretty terrific. You. The kids. It's what I want."

His marriage broke up because his wife couldn't have children. She and Mason were already parents. Annie did like him. A lot. It wasn't love, but that was so much better. Who needed drama and heartbreak? He was steady. Supportive. Sweet. She was happy around him and enjoyed spending time together. She looked forward to seeing him after work.

And there was that kiss.

"Come on, Annie." He took her hand and brushed his

thumb over her left ring finger. "This is the right thing to do."

Her exact words just a little while ago about letting him know he was a father. She waited for some sign, a knot in her stomach, a shred of doubt in her mind, something to make her say no way. But there was nothing. Just a feeling that this could work really well.

"Okay, Mason. I'll marry you."

Escrow on the house had closed less than a week ago so Annie had been busy helping Mason move things in. It had kept her too busy to be nervous about the wedding. But two weeks after his proposal they were going to take vows. Things had come together quickly, partly because it was small, partly because Florence Blackburne was a tireless volunteer on their behalf and wanted this to happen.

On Thursday evening two weeks after becoming engaged, Annie and Mason stood in front of someone who was licensed by the State of California to marry them. Flo had found him on the internet. He was a skinny twentysomething who looked like a college student earning extra money. Carla was her maid of honor; Mason's dad was the best man. His mom and sister held the babies, who looked completely adorable. Charlie had on a little black suit and red bow tie that he kept pulling off. Sarah was wearing a pink-tulle, cap-sleeved dress with a darker pink satin ribbon that tied in a big bow in the back.

If anyone thought Annie's tea-length red dress was an odd choice, they kept it to themselves. The bodice was snug-fitting chiffon and the full, flirty, asymmetrical midcalf hem flattered her figure. Muscle was building up in her leg but she was a little sensitive about it being thinner than the other one.

Patrick's Place had been closed for this private function. Carla was BFFs with the owner, Tess Morrow Wallace, and had facilitated the arrangements. Annie was aware that Mason had met his ex-wife here, but the interior was new so she chose to be superstitious about that, in a positive way.

Tables and chairs were arranged to form an aisle for Annie to walk down. Now the Blackburne family formed a semicircle around Annie and Mason in the center of the room. Together they had written their own vows to each other and she was glad there wouldn't be any surprises because the unexpected always had a way of being bad.

Annie cleared her throat to go first. "I, Annie Campbell, take you, Mason Blackburne, to be my husband, and father to Sarah and Charlie. You're a good, decent man who takes care of them and me. In front of everyone gathered here, I promise to honor and cherish you and put the family we're making today above all else."

In his black suit, Mason was more handsome than she'd ever seen him. The blue stripes in his silk tie brought out the intense color of his eyes in the best possible way. And his smile... Her heart fluttered and she wasn't sure if nerves had chosen this moment to trip her up or if it was something else a lot more complicated. He didn't touch her with any part of his body, but their gazes met and locked and made her feel as if he was holding her in his arms.

"I, Mason Blackburne, take you, Annie Campbell, for my wife. I solemnly promise to respect, honor and care for you and our children to the very best of my ability. It's good and right, and I look forward to making a family with you and Sarah and Charlie."

She and Mason exchanged plain gold bands, after which the internet guy said, "I now pronounce you husband and wife."

Neither of them moved and Gabriel Blackburne said, "Isn't this the part where you kiss the bride?"

Annie felt a quiver in her stomach and instinctively turned her face up to look at Mason. He smiled then slowly lowered his mouth as her eyes drifted closed. His lips were soft and chaste but that didn't stop memories of their first kiss from popping into her mind. This felt like a down payment on a promise for later. And it didn't last nearly long enough.

Mason pulled back and said, "Hello, Mrs. Blackburne. How do you feel?"

Good question. This was a done deal now. Legal. She'd made decisions in the past and instantly had second thoughts if not outright regrets. What-the-heck-have-I-done moments. But this wasn't one of them. Mason was all the good things a man should be and there was no denying that sparks happened every time he touched her. Most important, the babies would have their father and a normal life.

"I feel great," she said, smiling back at him.

"Me, too."

"Me, three." Carla hugged both of them. "Congratulations. You make a beautiful couple."

"I couldn't agree more." With Sarah in her arms, Florence gave her son a one-armed hug before doing the same to Annie. "Welcome to the family, sweetheart."

"Thank you." Unexpectedly, Annie's eyes filled with emotional tears. Her voice only caught a little when she said, "It's really nice to have a family."

The rest of the Blackburnes lined up to congratulate them. All but Gabriel, she noticed. The bar was open and he'd walked over for a drink. Then she was swept up in the celebration and Charlie was leaning toward her, wanting to be held. Sarah did the same to Mason.

He met her gaze and there was a tender look in his. "We're a family and as soon as the court recognizes me as their father, we'll be official."

"That won't be long," she said. "But I'm officially starving right now."

"Let's go eat. Mom—"

"On it, honey."

Adjacent to the main bar area was a restaurant where tables had been arranged in long rows to accommodate the family. Two high chairs had been set up on the end for the babies. Florence herded everyone to their assigned places, with Annie and Mason surrounded by their maid of honor and best man.

When they were all in place Flo said, "If Annie and Mason have no objection, I'd like to make the first toast."

He looked at her and she nodded. "Take it away, Mom."

"It gives me great pleasure to welcome Annie to our family. My son is a lucky man." She held up a flute of champagne. "Peace and long life."

Her husband frowned a little. "Isn't that from *Star Trek*?"

"Maybe, but it fits." Flo shrugged and nodded at him. "Okay, best man, it's your turn."

John stood and looked around the table. "It's a blessing to be surrounded by my children and grandchildren to celebrate this happy occasion. Mason, you're a lucky man. Annie, I'm very happy to have another daughter. Congratulations."

For the second time she felt emotion in her throat and tears gather in her eyes. She blinked them away and smiled at him. Everyone clinked glasses, and soon after food was served. There were many volunteers to help keep the babies occupied so that they could eat their wedding dinner without interruption. The meal was followed by a beautiful red-velvet cake garnished with roses around the base. Everyone was mingling, chatting and having a good time.

Then Annie and Mason somehow found themselves alone in the crowd. He had a glass of champagne in his hand and said to her, "So, I have a toast."

"Oh?"

"I'm not a man of words, so don't expect profound."

She smiled. "You do okay."

"Right." He held up his glass. "Here's to us."

"To us," she said, touching her glass to his. "It was a nice wedding."

"Agreed. But on the one-to-ten nice scale, that dress is a fifteen." There was more than a little male interest in his eyes. "Why red?"

"Symbolism and maybe a bit of superstition." She sipped her champagne. "Red can be a sign of good luck, joy, prosperity, celebration, happiness and long life."

He nodded and slid one hand into the pocket of his suit pants, striking a very masculine pose. "All good reasons. And not traditional."

She couldn't tell whether or not that bothered him. "I know we took this step to have a traditional family for the twins, but—"

"You think I'm upset that you didn't wear white?"

"Are you?" she asked.

"No. This couldn't be more different from my first wedding and that's a very good thing. Only—" It looked as if something had just occurred to him. "You've never done this before. It's a really bad time to ask. And, for the record, I'm an idiot for not thinking about it until just now. Are you okay with a small wedding?"

"If I wasn't, you'd have heard. In case you haven't noticed, I'm not shy about standing up for myself."

"Yeah, I figured that out the first time we met. And I quote, 'Do the swab and leave your contact information. Now please go.'"

"Yeah." She grinned. "Not my finest hour. In my defense, I was tired and the twins were teething."

"No, I get it. You're independent and it's one of the things I like about you. I just wanted to make sure you're fine with the size of this wedding because having something bigger would have meant waiting—"

"Speaking of that—" Gabriel Blackburne joined them and had apparently overheard. He had a tumbler in his hand containing ice and some kind of brown liquor. "Why didn't you?"

"Didn't we what?" Mason asked.

"Wait to get married."

Annie guessed Mason hadn't discussed with his brother why they'd decided to take this step. And she couldn't read the other man's expression. It wasn't animosity exactly, more like concern. There was also something dark and maybe a bit bleak, but she sensed that was personal to Gabriel and had nothing to do with her and Mason.

"Don't get me wrong." Gabriel took a sip from his glass. "I wish you both all the best. But why rush things?"

"It's about being a family," Mason explained. "My escrow closed. Annie and the kids were half moved out of her apartment because of the broken leg. It seemed a good time to merge households."

"A merger. My job is turning around failing businesses, but..." His brother's expression was wry. "Be still my heart."

"Annie and I talked this through and we agreed it was the best thing for the children. We want to give them a conventional home. Like you and I had."

"Yes, we did." Gabriel's expression grew just a little darker. "But a successful family starts with a strong core."

"It does," Annie said. "We are in complete agreement about the twins and raising them in a stable and loving environment."

"So you are in love?" Again he glanced at Annie but his gaze settled squarely on his brother. "Because if I'm not mistaken, you were never going there again."

Mason's eyes narrowed but his voice was even and casual when he responded. "Annie is the most courageous and warm woman I've ever met. And it seems to me that if you're this cynical, you aren't the best person to be working in a business that is supposed to help people find their life partner."

"You are so right. That's why my goal is to make that business profitable again as quickly as possible so I can leave." He finished the last of the liquor in his glass. "I'm not telling you anything you don't already know, but this 'merger' will change everything."

"For the better," Mason said.

Annie knew the man meant well but she shivered at the words. Before she could think that through, she recognized Sarah's tired cry and knew Charlie wouldn't be far behind.

"Mason, I think the grace period on the twins' good mood has just expired."

"Yeah."

"I sincerely wish you all the best," Gabriel said again. "You have a beautiful family. I envy you, brother."

Mason smiled and held out his hand. His brother took it then pulled him in for a bro hug. "See you Sunday at Mom's."

They said good-bye and went to retrieve their children from Mason's mother and father. Annie took Sarah and

Mason grabbed Charlie, who rubbed his face against his father's shoulder. It was a classic sign of being overtired.

"We need to get these guys home," she said to Florence.

"Why don't you two stay?" his mother said. "I can keep them at my house overnight."

And that was the exact moment it really sank in for Annie that being married *did* change everything. When you married a man, he became your husband and you were his wife. A couple. And couples had sex on their wedding night.

Chapter Nine

After his mother offered to keep the kids, Mason could have kissed the woman. A wedding night alone with Annie sounded just about perfect to him. Not that he didn't love his children to the moon and back, but... Taking that sexy red dress off his new bride sent his imagination and other parts of him into overdrive. There hadn't been a specific conversation about sex but after that kiss he figured they were good. If one of the babies hadn't interrupted them, their first time would already have happened.

But it felt right to have waited until after they were married. Right for Annie somehow. That was probably stupid, but that's the way he felt.

"What do you think?" he asked her.

Annie looked a little pale and her smile was forced. "That is so sweet and thoughtful. I can't thank you enough for the offer. But we got married to be a regular family. It doesn't seem right not to have them with us on our first night."

Mason had mixed feelings. He felt like biomedical waste because it crossed his mind that he wanted her all to himself. That made him a selfish jerk for not wanting to share her. The other part of him realized how important it was to get this right.

"We appreciate it, Mom. But I agree with Annie."

This was better, he told himself. No pressure on either of them. The twins came first and that meant bathing, feeding and rocking them to sleep. That might happen by midnight and they would fall into bed exhausted, too tired for... Anything.

Mason tried not to be disappointed and almost succeeded. Almost.

They bundled the kids into jackets because the October evening was chilly. Buckling them into the carriers that fit into the car was more of a challenge. Being overtired and out of sorts, they cried and fought the restraints, but he and Annie out-stubborned them.

She hugged his mom and dad. "Thank you for everything."

"You're so welcome, sweetheart." Flo smiled. "I think you'll make my son a happy man."

Annie glanced at him but her expression was impossible to read. "I'm glad you think so."

Mason looked around the pub's dining area and noticed a busboy busy loading dirty dishes from their dinner into a plastic tote. Still, he had to ask. "You're sure you don't need us for anything here?"

"No. We have it covered. Take your family home."

"I like the sound of that." He looked at Annie and she nodded. "Good night, all. Thanks for coming."

His parents had picked up Annie and the twins, so her car was at the house. They walked outside, each carrying a crying infant. Even after they were secured in the rear seat of his SUV the crying continued. It was impossible to have a conversation over the high-pitched wails. Fortunately it didn't take long to get home.

He pulled into the driveway beside her small, compact car. Annie opened the front passenger door and the overhead light came on.

"I'm glad they didn't fall asleep," she said.

"Why?" Because she didn't want to be alone with him? Was she trying to tell him something?

"Because I'd be tempted to put them to bed without even undressing them. They need baths, jammies and bottles. Never too soon to start a routine."

"Good point."

In the house they set Sarah and Charlie facing each other on the family room rug. The settling-in process was ongoing so boxes were scattered throughout and furniture was still scarce. Shopping for it hadn't been a priority. The babies' nurseries were put together, each with its own crib. But the cartons lined the walls in the rest of the rooms and needed to be unpacked.

Annie looked around ruefully. "Is this all my stuff or yours?"

"Fifty-fifty." He settled his hands on his hips, pushing back his suit coat. "And I have one more load from my storage unit."

She sighed. "It doesn't feel like we'll be settled anytime soon."

Was she trying to get a message across? Or was he reading too much darkness into that conversation with Gabriel tonight? Until then he'd felt just fine about this whole thing. Now... Time would tell.

The twins had been quiet since coming into the house, both of them looking around with wide eyes. Charlie rubbed his face, a sure sign of an imminent meltdown.

Annie saw it, too. "I'm going to get out of this dress."

It had been a long shot at best, but there went any chance of him sliding the sexy material off her. She was probably going to slip into something more comfortable but it would likely be sweatpants not lingerie. He wasn't proud of these thoughts, but he was a guy.

"Okay. I'll entertain them while you change for operation bath time."

"Roger that." She smiled then hurried out of the room.

Charlie's whimpers turned to full-blown wails, so Mason unbuckled him and lifted the little guy into his arms. That was Sarah's cue to commence with her own high-pitched vocal demonstration of unhappiness. She arched her back against the straps holding her in, but he didn't want to undo them and have her sliding out of the seat.

He put his son on the rug. *Don't judge*, he thought, grateful the germ police weren't around. He was getting a bath soon. Then he freed Sarah and cuddled her close for a moment while her brother took off on another crying jag.

Mason went down on one knee and put a hand on the boy's belly. "I honestly don't know how your mother did it all by herself."

"It wasn't easy." Annie had quietly entered the room and moved closer.

He looked up. "And yet somehow you made it look easy."

"I doubt that. But thanks." She held out her arms for Sarah. "Now, unless you want soap and water all over that nice suit, you should change into a slicker and rubber boots."

"Understood."

Mason put on jeans and a T-shirt, then grabbed his son off the floor and followed Annie into the bathroom that connected the twins' nurseries. Their small tub was already out on the counter by the sink and she filled it with warm water before handing her baby off to him. He had one in each arm and watched her set out two sets of PJs, diapers and two fluffy towels.

She took Sarah and stripped off the dress, tights and diaper before lowering her into the water. Little hands and feet started moving. Crying stopped and splashing started.

"They do love the water, but there's no playing tonight." Annie washed, rinsed and lifted Sarah out before quickly wrapping the towel around her.

Mason had removed Charlie's clothes while his sister was being bathed. They handed off babies and he took Sarah into her room and dressed her in the clothes Annie had put out. By the time he finished, Charlie was in a towel and on the way to his room. He stood in the doorway, holding his sweet-smelling daughter.

"Assembly line works like a charm," he said.

She looked up for a moment and smiled. "An extra pair of hands makes this so much easier."

"We make a good team."

"Yes, we do." She finished putting on Charlie's one-piece blue sleeper. After picking him up, Annie held him close and brushed a hand over his back while he rubbed his eyes again. "You're a tired boy. Let's give them a bottle and put them to bed."

"The same crib? Or their own?"

She met his gaze, thinking that one over. "I don't know. Thoughts, Doctor?"

"Not a pediatrician but… Sooner or later they have to be in their own rooms. This is a new environment anyway, so it might be a good time to try. The worst that could happen is they won't go to sleep and we put them in the same crib again."

Annie nodded. "And if it works, they might sleep

through each other's fussiness and we'd only have one awake at a time. That sounds too good to be true. But I vote we give it a try."

"It's unanimous," he said.

After bottles, the twins were asleep. They carefully put them in their respective rooms then met in the hall to wait for the crying to start. Five minutes went by and all was quiet. Annie held up two fingers, indicating they should give it another couple of minutes. They both held their breaths but there wasn't a sound.

She angled her head toward the family room and he followed her there. "I am cautiously optimistic that this just might work."

"A wild prediction."

"You're a pessimist," she scolded. And sure enough, ten minutes passed without a peep. "Cautious optimism rules. It would appear they're in for the night. What are we going to do with ourselves?"

Then her eyes widened and a blush covered her cheeks. Any other time the kids would have been fussy and out of sorts, but not now. It had been smooth and easy getting the twins to sleep, but Mason sensed a whole pile of awkward in the room. He knew her pretty well now and there was no question that Annie looked tense.

He had wanted her practically from the first moment he'd seen her and now she was his wife. But he'd been getting vibes from her and not the ones he was hoping for.

There were so many ways this could go sideways and he didn't want to do the wrong thing. He didn't want to be another jerk in her life. That was no way to start out. On the other hand, they *were* married. But one of them had to address this situation.

He cleared his throat. "Annie, you're probably really tired and—"

When he stopped and let the meaning of his words sink in, a charged silence joined the awkwardness dividing them like the wall that once separated East and West Berlin. Her eyes changed color, as if a light had gone out. But that was probably his imagination.

Finally she nodded. "It has been a long day—"

"Right. Sure."

She half turned toward the hall. "I think I'll turn in now."

"Okay."

When she was gone, Mason poured himself a Scotch and leaned against the island that overlooked a family room empty of furniture. If one was into symbolism, this would be a doozy. He had thought marrying her would solve problems and fill up his life. He'd had no idea it would be just the beginning of complications.

What was it she'd said? It was never too early to get into a routine. What did this say about the routine they were starting?

Annie barely slept on her wedding night but not for the reason she should have not slept. And a week later nothing had changed. They slept in the same bed but his long shifts at the hospital and caring for the twins became an excuse for him to avoid intimacy. The rejection hurt on many levels, but what stung most was her poor judgment. How wrong she'd been about the sparks between them. Well, half-wrong, anyway. She was the only one who'd felt them.

They had made legal promises to each other, not physical ones, but she'd assumed that would all work out based on one hot kiss. She'd made the first move then but desperately wanted him to make the first move now. Annie had her pride and didn't want him to sleep with her just because they'd said "I do." Or worse, pity.

She threw back the covers and went into the master bedroom's adjoining bath. Lingering humidity and the sexy male scent of cologne told her Mason had recently showered. Apparently she'd slept harder than she'd thought because she hadn't heard him. Obviously he'd taken care to be quiet. That was thoughtful and he got points, but her anger and hurt refused to budge.

After taking care of business, she checked on the twins and smiled tenderly at each of them still sleeping in their very own rooms. Little angels, she thought. They were safe, secure—loved. That's all that mattered, right? Right.

Still, quiet time was rare and she went down the hall toward the kitchen to make coffee and enjoy a peaceful moment before all hell broke loose. The hallway opened to the family room, which was adjacent to the kitchen. With his back to her, Mason was standing there in blue scrubs because he was on his way to work. She so didn't want to face him. Eventually she'd have to, just not right this minute.

But before she could scurry back to bed and pull the blanket over her head, he turned and spotted her. She froze, feeling like a deer caught in headlights.

"I'm sorry if I woke you," he said.

Don't be nice to me, she thought. *Just don't.* If he was, she would have to let go of her anger and let down the only shield she had to keep out the hurt scratching to get in. She also couldn't ignore him, no matter how ill at ease she felt.

Annie moved closer, trying to act as if all was fine and normal, but her legs felt stiff and trying to smile made her face hurt. "You didn't wake me."

"Good." He nodded a little too enthusiastically, signaling that he felt awkward, too.

She was in the kitchen, but kept her distance from him. "Charlie and Sarah are still asleep."

His gaze didn't quite meet hers. "They must be growing."

"I guess so."

After a few moments of tense silence he said, "I made coffee. Would you like a cup?"

"Yes. Thanks." This was so stiff, tense, awkward and overly polite, it made her want to scream.

He seemed relieved to have something to do and immediately took a mug from the cupboard above the coffee maker, then poured steaming hot liquid into it. Packets of her artificial sweetener were in a bowl on the counter and he ripped one open before shaking the powder in. Then he grabbed the container of flavored creamer from the refrigerator and poured that in, lightening the dark color to the exact shade she liked. The thoughtfulness was both incredibly sweet and super annoying. He held out the cup.

"Thanks," she said grudgingly. She took a sip and noted that it was perfect. This was probably where she should meet him halfway. "How late are you working tonight?"

"It's twelve hours, so seven to seven. Probably seven thirty-ish."

"Ish?"

"If an emergency comes in around change of shift, I could be delayed getting out. Every day is different. Why?"

"I was wondering about dinner."

"Right." He leaned back against the counter and folded his arms over his chest.

Annie swallowed against a sudden surge of overwhelming attraction for the man she'd married. She'd seen him in scrubs before as he'd often come by the apartment after work to see Charlie and Sarah. When they'd been living with his folks she'd seen him before he'd left for the hospital, too. In her opinion the lightweight top and pants looked comfortable, like pajamas, and weren't the sexiest ensemble in the world.

But the über masculine pose he struck drew her gaze to the contours of his chest and the width of his shoulders. She had the most powerful urge to be in his arms, held tight against his body. Except he'd shut the door on that and every night since then rejection grew wider and more painful.

"If you get hungry, go ahead and eat without me."

"Hmm?" What were they talking about? Her mind had gone completely blank.

"Dinner. Tonight. If I'm not home and you need to eat, don't wait for me."

"Okay. I'll make you a plate."

"Don't go to any trouble," he said. "And I'm sure I'll be home in time to help with baths."

"Right." A devoted dad. He wanted to help with the nighttime ritual. "Unless they're really fussy, I'll hold off until you get here."

"Great." Again with the enthusiastic nodding. He was going to give himself head trauma.

But again the sweet consideration irrationally ticked her off. It was official. She was crazy. "Okay, then."

She sipped her coffee and looked anywhere but at him. "If you have to leave for work, don't let me keep you."

"I have a few minutes."

She waited for him to say more but he didn't. Since you could cut the tension in the room with a scalpel, she would think he'd have jumped on her suggestion and hit the road. But, oddly, he seemed reluctant to leave. Of course, that was about his children, not her.

"Would you like some breakfast before you go?" It seemed wrong somehow not to offer.

"No. Thanks, though. I'll just grab something in the doctor's dining room. At the hospital," he added.

"Right. Because it's logical that the doctor's dining room would be at the hospital." Was she awful for not resisting the urge to tease him?

"This is what you might call a 'duh' moment." The corners of his mouth curved up, cracking the tension a little. For the first time, he met her gaze. "What's on your agenda for today?"

Look at him. Asking his wife what her plans were for the day. Just like any normal couple. If he could pretend, so could she.

"I'm going to the apartment to clean out the last of my things."

"You should let me help with that," he said.

How ironic was this? She was ending her old life at the same time she was dealing with the unforeseen fall-out from her new one.

"I gave my notice and have to be out." She wrapped her hands more tightly around the mug.

"But the cast hasn't been off your leg very long. Let me see if I can work something out and help—"

"It's all right." She was touched that his concern seemed genuine. But she was used to doing things alone. That was self-pity talking. She did have backup, just not from Mason. "I can handle it. Your mom is going to watch the twins. And Carla is meeting me there to help. She took a hooky day. Called in sick. Don't tell Gabriel."

"You think I'd rat her out when she's helping you?" It wasn't clear from his expression whether or not he was kidding. "I'm hurt that you think so little of me." He was talking about his male pride but her pain went a lot deeper than that. A place she'd thought was scabbed over and protected. A wound from childhood that she'd actively worked to heal and forget. As much as she wanted to blame him, it wasn't fair. They had moved quickly to marry. Between taking care of the babies and moving, they'd been so busy. Discussing the finer points of this arrangement hadn't been a priority.

"On the contrary, I think you're incredibly honest." She sincerely meant that. "And on the off chance you might run into your brother, it was simply a reminder not to say anything about Carla."

"My lips are sealed."

And so, apparently, was his heart. She needed to do the same. "Good."

He glanced at the digital clock on the microwave. "It's time. I really have to go."

"Have a good day." Wasn't she the world's most supportive wife?

"Hold down the fort while I'm gone." A husband's automatic response.

"Will do," she said.

He straightened away from the counter and hesitated for a moment. Annie had the feeling he was going to kiss her goodbye, a classic husband move, before heading off to work. She held her breath. But hope was a cruel thing because he didn't move close to her after all.

"I'll see you tonight." He turned away and headed for the front door.

Annie heard the soft click of it closing behind him and thought it was the saddest sound ever. On the way to his car in the driveway he would walk across the porch that had caught her heart and reeled in her hopes. It symbolized the dream for a traditional family that she'd had her whole life. But regret flooded her now because she knew all the front porches in the world couldn't fix what was wrong with this picture.

When she'd first met Mason, he hadn't trusted her, what with being the sister of the woman who hadn't told him he might be a father. And Annie hadn't believed he would stick around and take care of his children. They'd been wrong and had become friends, working side by side to care for the twins both of them loved more than anything. Taking the marriage step had seemed perfectly logical but she never dreamed it would create this awful divide between them. They were together legally but had never been further apart.

Chapter Ten

Annie climbed the stairs to her soon-to-be vacant apartment and bittersweet memories scrolled through her mind. Jessica announcing that she was pregnant and didn't know who the father was. The nervous and happy excitement when labor had started. The thrill of the twins' birth turning to fear and unimaginable grief because Jess died. Bringing the babies here when they were so tiny and she couldn't carry both of them up the stairs at the same time. The sheer terror of caring for both infants by herself.

Until Mason showed up and stood right here, she thought, looking at the familiar door. The moment she'd seen him, her life had changed in so many ways—some good, some not so much.

She unlocked the door and carried moving boxes and trash bags inside. The place was empty of furniture. Indentations in the carpet were the only clues that her couch and coffee table had once been there. Now they were in storage until decisions were made about what to do with everything. That seemed inconsequential considering everything else that was going on—or not going on.

"Hello."

Annie turned and Carla stood in the doorway with cups of coffee in her hands. "Hey, you. Thanks for coming."

"Doesn't look like you need much help," she said. "Mostly I came because you promised to take me to lunch."

It felt good to laugh and Annie was grateful to her friend for that. And the coffee. She took the to-go cup Carla held out. "The big stuff is gone, obviously. I need another pair of eyes to make sure I don't miss anything."

"I can do that." Carla looked around. "Where do you want to start?"

"The master bedroom." Also known as the room for sleep because in her world no one was being bedded.

Annie led the way and again only the marks on the rug indicated where the bed and nightstands had been. In the bathroom they set their coffee on the countertop between the two sinks. Annie opened the medicine cabinet while her friend got down in front of the cupboard underneath the sink.

"There's a shower cap here," Carla said. "A couple of gigantic hair rollers. A long-handled back scrubber. Nearly empty bottles of shampoo and conditioner."

Annie glanced away from what she was doing. "That was when I changed brands to get more volume. I kept those for an emergency."

"Do you want me to put these in a box?"

If only hair products would take care of her current crisis. Come to think of it, if she had better hair, maybe Mason would be attracted to her.

"Annie?"

"Hmm?" She pulled her thoughts back to what she was doing.

Carla held up the plastic bottles. "Keep or toss?"

"Throw them out."

"Done." She pulled out a trash bag and dropped the discards into it.

Annie took bottles out of the medicine cabinet and checked each label. There was one that said "Jessica Campbell." Prenatal vitamins. Her sister had wanted the cheapest over-the-counter brand but Annie had insisted she listen to her obstetrician, who'd said the prescription had the right amounts of what she needed for the baby. That was before she'd known there were two. A sob caught in her throat.

She'd been so busy with Charlie and Sarah that she hadn't had time to grieve, and an unexpected pain settled in her chest. It was emptiness and loss and missing the only person she'd ever truly been able to count on to love her.

"Are you okay?" Carla was staring at her.

"Why do you ask?"

"Oh, please. Your face is an open book. Never play poker, by the way. You suck at bluffing."

Annie handed over the bottle. "It just hit me all over again that she's gone and isn't coming back."

"Oh, sweetie—" Carla took it from her and closed her hand over the name. "I wish there was something I could say to make it better."

"Me, too. And I feel guilty."

"Why? You were there for her when she needed you most. And you took in her children without missing a beat." Carla sat back on her heels. "What could you possibly have to feel guilty about?"

"I love Charlie and Sarah with all my heart. They are the best thing that ever happened to me. But at what price?" Tears filled her eyes.

"Annie—" Carla stood, moved closer and hugged her.

"It's not like you made it happen. If you could bring her back, you'd do it in a heartbeat. And Jess wanted you to have the babies. She gave them to you."

"She didn't have a choice. I'm all she had and she's all I had. Our mother and her husband made it clear no help was coming from them. Not that it ever did. In a meaningful way anyhow."

"Their loss."

"And I'm sad that the babies will never know their mom. She was loyal and brave. She stood up for me when no one else would."

"You'll tell them about her," Carla said gently. "And all of her wonderful qualities aren't gone forever. They'll live on in her children."

"You're right." Annie's mouth trembled but she managed to smile. "I need to think about that."

"You haven't had much time or energy to think about anything. You've been treading water and getting by these last few months," her friend pointed out. "And life is give and take, yin and yang."

"I'm not sure where you're going with that."

"Losing your sister was horrible and tragic. But circumstances brought Mason into your life."

Just hearing his name made Annie's chest tighten, but not with sadness. It was way more complicated than that. "Yes. Mason is in my life."

Annie turned back to the medicine cabinet and pulled out a thermometer, antibiotic ointment, peroxide and Band-Aids. First aid supplies would fix a scrape but not what was ailing her.

It was quiet in the room and she'd been too lost in her own thoughts to realize Carla hadn't said anything in response to her Mason comment. In fact she could almost feel her friend's gaze locked on her like a laser beam.

She glanced over her shoulder and knew her inability to bluff was going to bite her in the butt. "What?"

"Something's bothering you. Something besides losing your sister."

Annie didn't want to talk about this but she faced the other woman and prepared to fake it. "No. I'm just tired. It's been hectic. First my leg. Moving in with Flo and John. Settling the kids. Moving again and cleaning out the apartment."

"Getting married." Carla leaned back against the sink. "How's that going, by the way?"

"It's an adjustment."

"Of course. But in a good way." Her eyes narrowed as she looked closer. "Right, Annie?"

"Yes. Of course—"

"Like I said. You suck at bluffing. Something is bothering you and for the life of me I can't figure out what could possibly be wrong. You just married a great guy. He's a hunk and a doctor. Is there any chance that your standards are just a little bit too high?"

Annie crossed her arms at her waist. "I'll admit that on paper my life looks perfect—good job, two beautiful, healthy children and a really hot husband…"

"But…?" her friend prompted.

Annie shrugged. "He doesn't want me."

"He married you."

"For his kids. To be a family. All of us under one roof for their sake."

Carla looked confused. "I really wish it was happy hour and this place had some furniture."

"What does that mean?"

"We could have wine and sit on a comfortable sofa for this chat." She picked up their coffee cups and slowly settled on the side of the tub, patting the space beside her. "This will have to do. Now sit."

Annie sat. "This isn't something girl talk can actually fix."

"Oh, ye of little faith. Besides, you won't know unless you try. I had no words of comfort for you losing your sister, but I've got plenty to say about you and Mason." Her friend was bossy, in a good way. "Now tell me what's going on. The truth. Don't hold back. What makes you think he doesn't want you?"

"He doesn't want to have sex with me."

Carla nearly spit out the sip of coffee she'd just taken. "Tell me I didn't just hear you say that your marriage hasn't been consummated yet."

"Yeah, that's exactly what you heard." Annie told her what happened on their wedding night.

"Okay. But think about this. Everything went down so fast. Maybe he was giving you time. It's possible he really is what he seems—caring and compassionate. That he was simply being a nice guy."

"It's been a week and he hasn't made a move. No guy is that nice." Annie had been miserable when she got here, but not like this. And, so far, talking things over was making her feel worse. "When he proposed, he said we liked each other, which is true. That we were friends, also true. But clearly he didn't mean anything more than that."

"How do you feel? Do you want to have sex?"

Annie thought about kissing him and he sure hadn't pushed her away. "Yes."

"Okay, then. Do something about it," Carla advised.

"Excuse me?"

"Come on to him. It's not the olden days. Things have evolved. Women can make the first move and not be a hussy."

"I can't. I've had enough rejection in my life. Enough humiliation. From Mason it would be—" Annie didn't have the words to describe what a no from him could do to her.

"Wouldn't it be better to know?" Carla asked gently.

Annie was dyslexic and school had been a challenge for her in more ways than one. She'd learned to compensate and be successful. Now her company was one of two finalists for the biggest contract they'd ever had and it was largely due to her vision and artistic execution of the campaign.

Intellectually she knew all of this but her inner child still heard the other kids ridicule her, tell her she was stupid, ugly, an idiot. School had been isolating and lonely, still she'd made it through. But Mason was honest. If she faced him outright and forced him, he would tell her the truth. That they were married friends without benefits. But could she handle hearing it?

"It probably would be better to know," Annie said. "I'll think about it."

Mason had to do something. The situation with Annie was tense and getting worse every day. And it was all his fault. After the problems in his marriage, then the divorce, followed by a year's deployment, he was apparently pretty rusty, socially speaking. He missed the easy conversation with Annie, the teasing and laughter. And the promise of that wedding kiss. But he'd blown it big-time.

So here he was at Make Me a Match. The office was in a building in the Huntington Hills business complex. He parked and exited the SUV, then walked through the double glass doors into the lobby with its elegant marble floor. The elevator opened when he pushed the up button, and he rode it to the top floor, where his aunt Lillian's business was located.

The elevator doors opened into a reception area with comfortable furniture arranged to facilitate conversation. Carla Kellerman sat behind the desk, and he knew she doubled as greeter and his aunt's assistant.

She looked up when he stopped in front of her. "Hey, Mason. How are you?"

"Fine."

"Really? You look terrible."

"Thank you." He felt that way, too, but tried to make a joke.

"Long hours at the hospital? Twins keeping you up at night?" There was an expression on her face: accusation mixed with pity.

"All of the above," he answered.

"How's Annie?"

"Great," he lied. He got the feeling she didn't buy the deception.

"To what do we owe this visit?" She toyed with a pen on her desk. "Since you got married—what was it, ten days ago?—I wouldn't think you'd be in the market to meet someone."

"I'm here to see Aunt Lil."

"I didn't see your name on her schedule. Do you have an appointment?"

"No." He was just desperate. "She was out of town and couldn't make the wedding. I haven't seen her for a while and just dropped by to surprise her. Maybe take her to lunch."

"Too bad. You just missed her," Carla said. "She had a lunch meeting."

Well, shoot, he thought. "My bad. I should have called first."

"Since you're here, do you want to say hello to Gabriel?"

Mason could truthfully say his brother was the last person he wanted to discuss this problem with. "That's okay. Don't bother him."

"Do you want to leave a message for your aunt?"

"Just tell her I was here and I'll talk to her soon." He lifted a hand. "Thanks, Carla. See you."

"Mason, is there anything I can help you with?"

She was Annie's good friend and the second-to-last person he wanted to talk to about this.

"No. It's all good. I'll just be going now—"

"Mason. What are you doing here?" His brother walked into the reception area from a side hall.

"Just stopped by to say hi to Aunt Lil, but she's not here. So I'm going to take off—"

"What's your hurry? Have you had lunch? I was just going to order takeout. Wouldn't mind some company. Come on back to my office."

"Okay." There was no way to make a graceful exit now. "Nice to see you," he said to Carla.

"You, too. Say hi to Annie for me." The woman looked as if she was going to say something more but instead she just smiled.

"Will do."

Mason followed Gabe to an office at the end of the hall. When both of them had walked inside, his brother closed the door.

"What's wrong?" he asked.

"That's direct."

His brother was wearing a T-shirt, jeans and sneakers. Mason had a hunch that, at least for today, his consulting work was strictly behind the scenes and not with clients.

"That's the way I roll. Now answer the question."

He stood in front of the abnormally tidy desk because there were no visitor's chairs in front of it. "Nothing is wrong. Why would you think that?"

Gabe rested a hip on the corner of his desk. "Because you've never dropped in to see Aunt Lil."

"I was deployed. It was a little difficult to commute for a drop-in," Mason said. "And how do you know that? You haven't been here that long."

"I've been here long enough to know that this visit is out of character for you."

"What do you know about character?"

"Okay." His brother looked down for a moment then gave him a wry look. "You're going to mock me because math and spreadsheets and data are my thing."

"Well, yes, that was my plan," Mason admitted.

"It's true that I'm not involved very much with the other part of this business. But since you've been back from deployment, you never just dropped by to see Aunt Lil at work. That's not criticism, simply a fact. From that data I can extrapolate that you have a problem and think our aunt is qualified to advise you. Since you so recently got married, I deduce your issue is in some way connected to your wife. I'm right, aren't I?"

Mason sighed. "You're not wrong."

"I'm listening," Gabe said.

Mason figured it was a symptom of his acute desperation that he was actually considering telling Gabe what was going on. The brother who'd warned him that he might be moving too fast and marriage would change everything.

"I want your promise that you won't discuss this with anyone else. Especially anyone in the family," he added.

"Are you serious? I can't promise that. I'm not a priest or lawyer ethically bound to keep our conversation in the

strictest confidence. No medical privacy issues, either."
Gabe's grin was a clear indication of just how much he
was enjoying this.

"Then I'm not going to tell you." Mason half turned
toward the door.

"Okay. You win. My lips are sealed. But at least can I
have an 'I told you so'?"

"I think you just did." Mason hoped he didn't regret
this. "Now I want you to swear that you won't reveal to
anyone what I'm going to talk about."

"Like swear on a Bible?"

"On the bond of brotherhood," Mason said.

"That's really deep." His brother made a cross over his
heart. "You have my solemn promise."

"Okay." Mason blew out a breath. "I messed up with
Annie. On our wedding night."

"Dear God, Mason. I'm probably not the best person
to help with that. And, for crying out loud, performance
in bed is not in Aunt Lil's wheelhouse, either. Maybe you
should see a doctor—"

"It's not *that*." Once again Mason was reminded that
he was a healer and not so good with words.

"What a relief. So it's not sex—"

"It kind of is."

Gabe shook his head. "Just tell me what happened."

"Everything was fine when we left after the wedding.
We got the twins settled pretty fast. They were both sound
asleep at the same time, which almost never happens. It
was just Annie and me—" When his brother gave him a
get-to-the-point scowl, Mason said, "I was trying to be
sensitive. All the men she's known are jerks and I didn't
want to be another one. I didn't want her to feel pressure
to…you know—"

"Sleep with you?"

For now Mason ignored the irony of a doctor being reluctant to use the words. "It was supposed to be an out if she wanted one."

"What did you say?"

"That she was probably tired."

Gabe gave him a pitying look. "I'll admit I'm better with financial facts than women, but even I know not to tell a woman how she feels."

"I found that out." Mason would never forget the look in her eyes. Emotions had swirled but he'd had no idea what they were. He'd only known that at that moment everything between them changed. In a bad way. "The thing is, it's awkward and tense now. I don't know how to fix it. Doing the wrong thing could be worse than doing nothing at all."

"I had no idea." Gabe shook his head.

"What?"

"That you suck this bad at romance."

"Now you know," Mason snapped.

"I guess I'm not the only Blackburne who focuses on data and logic instead of emotions."

"If this was an emergency room and you were having a heart attack, I'd know exactly what to do. I'm stethoscope and chest tubes, not a matters-of-the-heart guy."

"I get it."

Mason met his gaze. "Since you just admitted you know very little about women, it's quite possible that I just bared my soul and humiliated myself for no reason. You can't help." Mason started pacing. "You're useless."

"I wouldn't go that far. At least, not completely useless." Gabe looked thoughtful. "I try to avoid the interpersonal part of the business but it's impossible to work here and not absorb some things."

"Such as?"

"How to set a romantic scene." His brother shrugged. "We arrange a lot of first dates. I hear things."

"In my case, it seems a lot like shutting the barn door after the horse got loose."

"Ah, yes. You've already met someone and married her." Gabe nodded. "You moved so fast, I have to ask. Have you ever actually taken Annie out? On a date, I mean?"

"It's been hectic," Mason defended. "We have two babies. Then she broke her leg. It's not easy to align everything for alone time."

"Making the most of what you've got is another conversation and not my point anyway. But there are things you can do to maximize the moments you do have."

"Such as?"

"Bring her flowers. Put rose petals on the bed. A bottle of champagne chilling in the bedroom." Gabe threw up his hands. "Google 'romantic gestures.' Because that's all I've got. Or you can ask Mom."

"I'm going to pretend you didn't just say that." Mason barely held back a wince.

"Too far?" Gabe grinned. "But you must see where I'm going with this."

"You're talking about courting her."

"Finally the clouds part and the light shines through." Then his smile faded, replaced by a lost and angry look. "I'm not sure of the rules anymore, but it used to be a kiss good-night on the first date."

"I've already kissed her," Mason said.

"Before the wedding?"

When he nodded, Gabe asked, "And?"

"Hot. Very, very hot."

"Good, you've got some game. On the second date, more kissing and touching. If that works, seal the deal on the third date." Gabe's expression was ironic. "I can't help pointing out that this is something you should have taken care of before the vows."

Mason glared at his brother. "I've lost count. You've said 'I told you so' how many times now?"

"Sorry."

"No, you're not." But Mason laughed.

"No. I'm not." Then Gabe turned serious. "I like Annie a lot. And those kids are terrific."

"You'll get no argument from me."

"I really wish you luck, Mason."

"Thanks." They shook hands and Mason pulled him into a bro hug. "I have to go. Things to do."

And a first date to plan.

Chapter Eleven

Annie left work later than usual, partly because a deadline was approaching and she'd felt the need to put in more time on her graphics for the new contract presentation. Partly to avoid Mason. He was off today and had taken over childcare while she'd gone to the office. Now she had to go home. It took so much energy to be chipper and "normal" when she felt anything but and she didn't have the sparkle to spare.

In spite of that, her heart always skipped a beat when she saw him. Tired after a long hospital shift. First thing in the morning, all rumpled and scruffy. Playing with the babies. When they worked together taking care of Sarah and Charlie, the tension went away and everything was like it used to be before they were married. But when they were alone...

Was Carla right? Should she come on to him? She was too oomph-depleted to think about it right now.

She guided her car onto the street where she'd lived only a short time and a knot tightened in her stomach. After pulling her compact car into the driveway and parking, she got out then opened the rear passenger door to retrieve her laptop case from the seat.

She walked to the front door and sighed with satisfaction over her porch. She did love it. Bracing herself, she went inside and made her way to the back of the house. It was eerily quiet. No baby coos, chatter or even crying. That was weird.

She moved into the kitchen, where Mason was at the counter, his back to her. It was a broad back, wide shoulders. And if things were different between them, she would march over and let herself feel those muscles for herself.

He turned and smiled. "I thought I heard you come in."

That grin was like a direct hit to her midsection and the shockwaves went through her whole body. "H… Hi."

"You had a long day." He glanced at the case in her hand and moved close. "Let me take that for you."

"What?" His hand closed over hers and held on maybe a little longer than necessary before he took it and her purse. "Oh… I can—"

"I'll just put these over here on the floor in the family room."

The manly scent of his skin had her senses reeling with awareness and she missed it when he moved away. Although distance allowed her brain to start functioning again.

"Where are the twins?"

"Asleep." He walked back into the kitchen and went to the bottle of wine sitting on the granite countertop. It was already open and breathing. He poured some of the deep burgundy liquid into two stemless glasses then handed one to her.

"They're actually asleep?" she asked.

"Yeah. No nap today, which I kind of planned." He

moved close and looked down at her. "We did errands. Then I took them for a long stroller ride in the park and they got lots of fresh air. They were tired and fussy for baths, but it worked out."

"You bathed them, too?"

"Yeah. You've been working hard. I knew you'd be tired."

She had been but right now not so much. This new and different Mason had her attention. After a sip of wine she said, "I better get dinner started."

"I already did. It's not fancy," he said. "Salad, twice-baked potatoes and steaks. I'll grill them."

"Wow." This couldn't be real. She must have stumbled into an alternate reality. "That sounds great. I'll set the table."

"Already done."

She glanced over at her small dinette set in the nook. There was a bouquet of flowers in the center and her heart simply melted. She could feel liquid warmth trickling through her as she stared at the white daisies, baby's breath and strategically positioned yellow roses. She walked over and leaned in to smell the sweet, floral fragrance.

"Mason, they're beautiful."

"Did you know that there are meanings attributed to different colored roses?"

"I think I heard that somewhere, but I'm a little surprised that you know."

"I got quite the education at the florist."

Her eyes widened. These weren't just an impulse buy at the grocery store? "You made a special trip?"

"Yeah. The twins won over everyone in the place and I think that got me extra attention."

The babies might have helped a little, but a man as incredibly good-looking as Mason would get attention from women if he was alone. "I'm pretty clear on the significance of red and white roses. But not yellow."

"According to Cathy, of Flowers by Cathy, it means joy, friendship and the promise of a new beginning."

Be still my heart, she thought. Then her practical self shut down any deeper implication. He probably just liked the color.

"They're really beautiful. So cheerful. Thank you."

"You're welcome." He moved to where she stood by the table and held up his wineglass. "What should we drink to?"

The sounds of silence surrounded her and she smiled. "Our healthy babies."

"To Charlie and Sarah." He touched his glass to hers and they sipped. "You must be starved. I'll cook the steaks."

"I'll toss the salad and warm the potatoes."

He shook his head. "You worked today. And this is our first— This is a…" He hesitated then finally said, "This is my chance to pamper you."

"And I appreciate it." More than she could say. "But I think you worked harder today than me. Like a wife."

His eyebrows rose. "That's high praise."

"I mean it." And she was grateful, from the bottom of her heart.

"I'm happy to do it." Intensity glittered in his eyes. Even though no part of their bodies touched, she felt as if he was touching her everywhere.

"And I'm happy to help. But before I do, I'm going to peek in on the twins."

She saw the baby monitor on the counter and they would hear if there was a problem, but she needed to see them. They grounded her and she needed grounding after Mason's sweet thoughtfulness. That made her feel like an ungrateful witch and she didn't mean to be. But she had a hard time trusting the good stuff.

She looked in on Charlie first and smiled at the soundly sleeping boy. He was on his back, arms and legs out-stretched as if he appreciated having space all to himself. She couldn't resist brushing a silky blond strand off his forehead and, fortunately, it didn't disturb him.

Then she tiptoed into Sarah's room. The little girl was a tummy sleeper, no matter how they tried to keep her on her back. Annie put a kiss on her finger and touched it gently to the little girl's round cheek. When Sarah moved, Annie froze. After all Mason's efforts, the last thing she wanted was to wake up this baby. She waited a few mo-ments and all was peaceful, so she quietly backed away.

Annie headed to the kitchen, where the French door was ajar. Through the glass she could see Mason watch-ing over the gently smoking grill. The hunter/gatherer, she thought. Today he'd hunted and gathered the heck out of their survival and she didn't know what to make of it.

By the time the steaks were ready she had the salad bowl and potatoes on the table along with the flowers and wine. It suddenly felt very romantic, in spite of the bright, canned light shining down. They sat across from each other and smiled.

"No candles?" she teased.

"Damn, I knew I forgot something." He actually looked upset with himself.

"Oh, my gosh. I was kidding, Mason. This is amaz-ing. I love it."

"Really?"

"Are you serious? I didn't have to cook it. That makes everything fantastic, like going out to dinner."

"Medical school was no culinary institute, so I didn't

learn how to serve elegantly. My service in the army neglected that, too."

"Now you're just fishing for compliments," she said.

"Did it show? And I thought I was being subtle." He grinned then said, "Try your steak. I wasn't sure how you like it. I did both medium-rare and figured I can cook yours more if you want."

"No. Medium is good." She made a cut and looked at the warm, pink center. "This is perfect."

The meat practically melted in her mouth, it was so tender. Suddenly she really was starving and practically inhaled the food and the rest of the wine in her glass.

Feeling the need to explain, she said, "I didn't have time for lunch."

"As a doctor I have to tell you that's not good."

"I was on a creative roll. Doing the last tweaks before we present our concept to the client." She shrugged. "I don't like all my eggs in one basket, which doesn't help."

He refilled her wineglass and she was reaching out when he set it down. Their fingers brushed. The touch was electric and she was sure something sparked in his eyes, too.

He cleared his throat. "What does that mean? All the eggs in one basket?"

"I don't put my creative energy into one concept. It's important to have a choice. So the team brainstorms two or three and we work them up. If we get the contract, the client will choose a direction and we'll put all the detail into that. But there will be enough that they can visualize each one."

"That's two or three times the work for you."

"It's an investment in our reputation. 'The company that works twice as hard for you.'" She rested her arms on the table and smiled.

"Something tells me you're a girl who puts maximum effort into everything, not just the job."

"I always try my best. Even when I was a little girl."

"And your parents didn't see the effort."

"You remembered," she said. A man who listened. It might be his most attractive feature.

"It's their loss. In case I haven't said it before."

She sighed. "Someday maybe I'll believe that. In the meantime, I don't want to lose out on moments with Charlie and Sarah. But I have to find balance. Being able to work remotely helps. And what you did tonight."

"Just pulling my weight," he said modestly.

Of which he had a lot, all muscle and temptingly male. And this change in him just might be leading somewhere exciting. Was she a fool to hope?

"Speaking of cooperation, I'll do the dishes since you cooked."

"Not in my restaurant," he said.

"At least let me help. It's the least I can do."

He thought that over. "Okay."

Together they cleared the table. Since there were no leftovers, it was only plates, utensils and a salad bowl. They finished wine while working and Annie was super relaxed and hyperaware. When their hands brushed exchanging plates, her breath caught. Their shoulders touched and her heart started to pound. She saw his eyes darken with something sexy and wild and she was almost positive it wasn't just her feeling this.

Should she jump his bones?

Fear froze her. If he didn't want her, she could lose even this, and she couldn't bear that. It was selfish, but also for the babies. Together they could provide a stable environment. More selfish, she didn't know what she would do without him or the family she finally had because of him. No, if a move was going to be made, he was the one who would have to do it.

When they were finished, he looked down at her. "I had a really nice time tonight."

"Me, too."

He looked away for a moment then met her gaze. "Would it be okay if I kissed you good-night?"

That was sweet and gentlemanly, almost as if they'd just met and… Was this a date? She smiled and nodded.

The corners of his mouth curved up as he cupped her face in his big hands then touched his lips to hers. The contact was soft and sweet and perfect. Tender and gentle, a gesture of promise.

He pulled back and there was a dash of regret in his eyes when he let her go. "I've got paperwork to do, so I'll say good-night. Sleep well, Annie."

All she could do was nod. She was breathless and wanting and more than a little disappointed. But she knew rejection and this wasn't it. Mason was up to something.

After working three days in a row at the hospital, Mason finally had two days off and planned to put Operation Courting Annie into high gear. He had taken the twins to his parents' house and, after carrying them inside, had gone back to the SUV for diaper bags, favorite blankets and stuffed animals they couldn't get along without.

He put the provisions in the room where the cribs were set up, the same one where Annie had slept. The thought of her sent heat rolling through him. Dinner and flowers had gone well and he had every reason to hope that tonight would, too.

Back in the family room, the babies were on a blanket and Lulu sat patiently between them while they awkwardly patted her furry back. His mom and dad sat on the floor with the kids and the dog; it was a modern Norman Rockwell moment.

Flo stood and walked over to stand beside him. "It feels like forever since I've seen these babies."

"You see them almost every day."

"But it's not the same as having them here," she said wistfully.

Mason watched his daughter crawl over to her grandfather and into his lap. Watching the man who'd raised him cuddle and interact with his own little girl tugged at his heart. He'd been too young to really remember this amazingly gentle and patient side of his dad, so it was cool to see now.

"Mason?"

"What?" He reluctantly looked away and focused on what his mother was saying.

"I said, where is Annie?"

When he'd called to make sure it was okay to bring the kids over, his mom had been on the phone with someone else. She'd confirmed they weren't busy and would love to babysit the twins. Then she'd cut him off. Now she wanted details.

"Annie is at the office, working."

"So why am I watching your children? Not that I mind."

"No, you're just nosy." He appreciated the fact that she didn't interfere but was deeply committed to knowing whatever was shared willingly. "The thing is, I'm going to surprise her at work and take her out to dinner." When you were raised by Florence Blackburne, a guy knew when he messed up and when he did good. This time he'd definitely done good.

"Oh, Mason, that's a wonderful idea. Very sweet and thoughtful of you."

And selfish. But he hoped it would be positive for both him and Annie. He also chose not to share that he'd actually taken his brother's advice and searched the internet for romantic gestures. Since he couldn't sweep her away to Fiji, surprising her at work followed by a dinner out, with candles this time, would have to do.

"I'm glad you approve, Mom." He looked at his father, who had been listening in. "Any objections, Dad?"

"Nope." He let Sarah pull the cell phone from his shirt pocket and grinned at her. "Say hi to Annie for us."

"You know it's Friday. Your father and I aren't working tomorrow. We can keep Charlie and Sarah overnight. If you'd like."

He had been hoping she would offer. Another piece of the plan clicked into place. "I'd appreciate it, Mom. And I know Annie will, too. Thanks."

"Anytime."

Lulu barked once and drew Mason's attention to Charlie pulling himself to a standing position right in front of the DVD stack.

"Red alert," he said.

"We're going to have to move those." His mother hurried over to grab up her grandson. "Come to think of it, babyproofing this house is now a major priority."

He kissed her cheek. "I have to go or my plan to intercept her before she heads home will be a dismal failure."

"Don't you worry. We'll take good care of these little angels." She gave Charlie loud kisses on his neck and he giggled.

"I'm sure the three of you will do fine with them."

"Who's the third?" she asked.

He pointed to the dog. "Lulu. In fact, Annie and I would like to borrow her."

"That dog does love these little ones," his mother agreed. "Now go. We've got this."

"Roger that."

He shook his father's hand and kissed the kids. And, this was a first, he got them to imitate his farewell wave. One of them said what sounded like "Bye-bye" and he'd swear on a stack of Bibles that it was first words.

Part two of his plan was officially in motion, he thought as he drove to Annie's office. It didn't take long and he parked in the lot that had more cars at this hour on a Friday night than he'd figured. Probably not all of them worked at C&J Graphic Design, but that didn't matter. The very definition of surprise meant you had to be flexible in the execution of the plan.

He walked into the lobby, pushed the up elevator button and the doors instantly opened. After getting inside and selecting the floor where her office was located, the nerves hit. What if she thought this was a stupid idea? What if he embarrassed her? And the worst: What if she had no desire to be anything more than what they already were?

The doors opened and across from him there was nothing but glass, the center etched with the words "C&J Graphic Design." He exited the elevator to get a better look at her office. He could see wood floors and cubicles divided by more glass. A doctor could do delicate surgery in this room what with the excellent track lighting overhead. All the workspaces were empty, except two.

Mason saw Annie standing just outside her cubicle, talking to a man who was outside the one next door. He looked to be in his early thirties, black hair and dark brown eyes that kind of smoldered. Surprise. Mason could have gone forever not knowing she worked with a guy good-looking enough to be on the cover of *GQ* magazine.

"No guts, no glory," he mumbled as he pushed open one of the heavy doors and walked inside, moving toward the twosome.

"Who are you?" Smoldering Eyes asked.

Annie turned and her eyes widened. "Mason!"

"Hi." He lifted a hand in a wave and stopped beside her.

"What are you doing here?"

"I wanted to surprise you and take you out to dinner." He met the other man's dark, curious gaze, then looked back at her. "Surprise."

"Mission accomplished. I'm definitely surprised." There was a pleased expression on her face before it slipped a little. "Where are the kids?"

"At the house. They'll be fine by themselves." He grinned to let her know he was kidding. "I had you for a second."

"No." But she playfully slugged his arm. "Seriously, where are they really?"

"Three guesses."

"Your parents'."

"Right in one," he said.

"So there really is a husband?" *GQ* asked.

"Yes." Annie looked apologetic. "Sorry. I should have introduced you. Mason Blackburne, this is Cruz Wright, one of my coworkers."

Mason shook the other man's hand. "Nice to meet you."

"Likewise. So you're the twins' father, the dad who got Annie to say yes."

Was there a hidden message in those words? Had this guy been planning to move in on her when Dwayne the Douche was out of the picture? Unclear.

"I am that man, yes." Mason moved close enough that

his arm brushed Annie's. Meeting her coworker gave him one more reason to be glad that she could do a lot of work remotely.

Just then an attractive young woman joined them and looked him up and down. "So, who's this?"

"Mason Blackburne, my husband." Annie looked up at him. "This is Ella Lancaster, my boss's assistant, and the woman who keeps things running smoothly around here. And she does it with extraordinary grace and good humor."

He shook her hand. "A pleasure, Miss—"

"Ella." She smiled. "Annie's been through a lot in the last year. We were happy for her when she told us she was getting married. It's about time someone lived up to Annie Campbell's rigorous standards."

"She doesn't suffer fools," Cruz explained.

"I suffered Dwayne." Annie glanced up at him and made an "eek" face. "Calling him a fool is an insult to fools."

"Right on." Cruz studied Mason. "Points to you for sticking around."

"He came to surprise me," she explained to Ella.

The other woman sighed and said to him, "Are there any more at home like you?"

"As a matter of fact, there are," Annie said. "He has two brothers. And a sister."

At the end of the row of offices, a door opened and a man emerged. He was in his fifties. Blond hair with gray at the temples, the lean body of a runner. He joined the group.

Before he could say anything Annie said, "Bob, this is my husband. Mason, this is Bob Clemens, our boss."

The man held out his hand. "Glad to meet you, Mason."

"Same here, sir."

"Annie says you were in the army. Deployed overseas recently."

"Yes, sir. I was assigned to a medical unit in Afghanistan."

"Thank you for your service." Bob looked around the group then settled his gaze on Mason. "To what do we owe the pleasure of this visit?"

"I'm here to surprise Annie and take her to dinner."

The man nodded his approval. "She's been working a lot of hours and deserves some quality downtime. The campaign for the client is ready and she needs to relax and have some fun."

"R and R, that's my plan," Mason said.

"Then what are you waiting for?" Bob asked. "Get her the heck out of here."

"Yes, sir." Mason looked down at her and held out his arm. "Let's go."

There was no hesitation or awkwardness when she put her hand in the crook of his elbow. She looked luminous and happy, and that gave him hope that he wasn't messing this up beyond repair.

Now for the next part of his plan.

Chapter Twelve

Annie was literally quivering with excitement as she walked out of the office on Mason's arm. Whatever was going on with him, she was giving this new attitude two thumbs-up and a double arm pump. Inside, of course. It took a lot of concentration to not giggle like a schoolgirl and walk normally. And he looked so sexy and handsome in his jeans, white dress shirt and sports coat. He was out of her league, but she would deal with that insecurity at another time.

Waiting for the elevator, she could feel her coworkers staring through the glass. Mason hadn't picked her up and carried her out in front of every employee, but it still felt like *An Officer and a Gentleman* moment.

She started to slide her fingers from his arm, but he put his hand over hers to keep it there. She smiled up at him.

"This is a very nice surprise."

"I'm glad."

"To what do I owe—?"

Before she could finish her question, the elevator doors opened and they walked inside. Mason pushed the button for the first floor and the ride down was fast. When they stepped out into the lobby, it was as if happiness made her see everything brighter and more clearly. Nothing was there that hadn't been there this morning, but that was before Mason had made the effort to surprise her at work.

In the corner by the tall glass windows there was a grouping of pumpkins, pots of rust-colored mums and a scarecrow announcing that fall was in full swing.

"This will be the twins' first Halloween," she said. "Should we take them trick-or-treating?"

"Affirmative." He glanced at the decorations and let his gaze wander over the whole lobby. "The little kids in costume are the best."

"I know. And it will be really different for me this year."

"Really?" He gave her a wry look. "You think? With two babies?"

"And a house. There aren't a lot of kids in my apartment building, but now I live in an actual neighborhood." She grinned. "It's going to be fun giving out candy and seeing all the costumes on the little ones."

"Logistics," he said thoughtfully.

"What?"

"Tactical operations center."

"You're going to have to translate that into nonmilitary terms for us civilians."

"One of us will have to stay home—tactical operations center or TOC—and give out that candy, while the other takes the twins around."

"Divide and conquer," she said, nodding.

"Right."

She sighed happily. "From my perspective that is a quality problem to have."

"I completely agree." He looked down at her, more carefree than the solemn, serious guy who'd knocked on her door to take a DNA test. "But the night is young and I'm starving. We can talk about this at dinner."

After walking outside into the cool, crisp evening air, she said, "My car is over there. I'll meet you at the restaurant. Where are we going?"

"Nope. It's top secret. I'll drive. We can get your car later." He pointed. "Mine is right there in the first row."

"Okay." At that moment she was ready, willing and able to go with him wherever he wanted to take her.

They strolled over to his SUV and he opened the door for her, handing her inside. For a split second, their faces were millimeters apart. She could feel his breath on her cheek and thought he was going to kiss her. And she wanted him to so very much. The streetlight illuminated his features and there was a hungry intensity there that had nothing to do with food. So when he didn't touch his mouth to hers, it wasn't a soul-wrenching blow. As he'd said, the night was young and they were going to dinner. As surprises went, this one was moving its way into her top five.

He got into the driver's seat and turned on the SUV, then guided it out of the lot to merge with street traffic. It was a little congested right now as a majority of people left work and headed home. She actually had no idea of their final destination.

"So, where are you taking me?"

"Like I said, it's a surprise."

"I thought you showing up unexpectedly at my place of employment was the surprise."

"Part of it," he confirmed.

"But I can't change your mind about keeping the dinner location a top secret?"

"Nope. Although, you'll figure it out soon enough. Short of blindfolding you, I can't keep it clandestine all the way there."

But how sweet was it that he was doing it at all? Annie

pinched herself, just to make sure she wasn't dreaming. The tweak on her wrist told her she wasn't.

As he drove, making left and right turns, the area became more open, less dense with single-family homes and zones where there were businesses and strip mall shopping. Finally, when he turned onto Summit Highway, she knew.

"Le Chêne," she whispered reverently.

"Affirmative."

It was one of Huntington Hills' most highly rated and exclusive restaurants. Upscale, cozy, romantic, historic. She'd only been there once. It was a spontaneous decision Dwayne the Douche had made without a reservation for the busiest place in town. They'd been turned away. So she knew the restaurant was located on a country estate and vineyards. When they slowly drove closer, she recognized the ivy-covered stone exterior that was reminiscent of a French château.

"This place is hard to get into," she said.

"I made a reservation."

Planning ahead, she thought. It was a very sexy quality.

He parked in the lot, then got out and came around to open her door. When she slid to the ground, he put his hand to the small of her back as they walked inside. The interior was dimly lit and had elegant oak wood beams and recessed lighting. The hostess confirmed a reservation for Dr. Mason Blackburne and showed them to a table for two in a secluded corner. There were candles on the table and that made Annie smile.

Tables were covered with pristine white tablecloths and the chairs were oak. It was country elegance with a wall full of wine bottles and lots of wood-framed mirrors.

The server came right over. "My name is Shelly. Can I get you something to drink?"

Mason asked for a wine list and picked out a bottle.

Shelly left menus and promised to be back in a few minutes. It didn't take long and she opened the red blend then poured a small amount in a long-stemmed glass for him to approve. He did and she filled both of their glasses before promising to return to take their orders.

"Let's drink to good surprises always," he said.

Annie touched her elegant crystal glass to his and heard a bell-like tinkling sound. "I can get behind that in a big way."

She took a sip of the dark red liquid and savored the perfect blend of flavors. "This is nice. Thank you for all of this, Mason."

"I have to apologize."

"For bringing me here to this beautiful place?"

"No. For not bringing you sooner," he said.

"You have nothing to be sorry for," she insisted.

"I disagree." He met her gaze across the small, intimate table and the flame in his eyes burned as brightly as the candles between them. "Everything was rushed and clumsy. The house. The wedding. Our first night. It was fast—"

"Is this your way of saying you're having second thoughts?" A familiar knot of apprehension tightened in her stomach. "Do you regret everything?"

"No," he said quickly. "Good God, no."

"Then what?"

"I'm trying to make it up to you."

"And I'll try to communicate my feelings," she said. "You can't read my mind."

"No, but I can read your face. There's been tension between us and it's my fault. I hope this is a new beginning."

Their server, Shelly, returned and took their orders. White sea bass for her and red snapper *meunière* for him. "Are you celebrating anything special?"

"No," Annie said.

"Yes," he said at the same time. "We just got married. No time for a honeymoon and we have twins. But this is a special occasion for us."

"Congratulations," Shelly said. "The twins. Boys or girls?"

"One of each," he said proudly. "This dinner is to celebrate the beginning of our life as a family."

"That's so sweet," the server said. "I'm a sucker for romantic gestures."

Me, too, Annie thought.

When they were alone she cleared the emotion from her throat and said, "So, Halloween logistics."

"Right, it occurs to me that my folks could help. Give out candy at the house while we take the twins out. They won't last long anyway, and it's not like they can eat candy."

She nodded. "Just a symbolic gesture, for pictures and the promise of future family traditions."

"I like the sound of that."

They chatted, laughed and teased until the food came. Everything was delicious and she knew that because he shared his with her and she did the same with him. The service was impeccable and Shelly brought them a piece of cheesecake topped with strawberries, on the house, to memorialize this dinner for them. He paid the bill and they walked outside, complaining about how full they were.

At the SUV Annie hesitated before getting in. She looked up at him and had no idea what he saw in her eyes, but on the inside she was brimming with joy. She couldn't ever remember being this happy.

"Thank you, Mason. I had a wonderful time. I feel like Cinderella and my coach will turn into a pumpkin if I don't leave the ball before midnight."

"This night doesn't have to end," he said softly.

"It does. We have to pick up the twins."

"My folks offered to keep them tonight. I made an executive decision and took them up on it."

Annie knew what he was saying and smiled. "For the record, I'm not tired at all."

"Yeah." He looked sheepish and so darn cute. "That was definitely not my smoothest moment."

"Past history." Annie threw herself into his arms and hugged him then turned her face up to his. He kissed her until she was breathless and finally she said, "I like your executive decisions. Now take me home."

"Can't this thing go any faster?" Annie was in the passenger seat of Mason's SUV. She was only half kidding but the lights from the dashboard illuminated Mason's grin.

"It *can* go faster actually, but I'd be breaking speed-limit laws. I don't know about you, but getting stopped by a cop right now isn't high on my to-do list."

"Mine, either, darn it." She looked at his profile, outlined by passing lights, and admired the straight nose, strong jaw. He was a handsome man, but beauty was only skin-deep. A pretty face didn't reveal character, but what he'd done tonight definitely did. "Mason?"

"Hmm?" He glanced over then returned his attention to the road.

"In case I forget to tell you later, tonight was the nicest surprise I've ever had. No one has ever done something so special for me."

"I'm full of the unexpected," he declared proudly.

Something in his tone caught her attention. It was mischievous, playful. "What?"

"Just stating a fact." Same roguish tone.

"You have something else up your sleeve," she said. "Give it up."

"You are so impatient."

"If I agree, will you tell me?"

"No."

"That's just mean," she said.

He smiled, completely unmoved by her words. "You'll thank me later."

"I guess I'll just have to trust you on that."

"And that's okay," he said softly. "You can."

Trust was the very hardest thing for her to do. Everyone in her world had let her down. Everyone but Jess. Except, in the end, she'd left, too. Not by choice, by fate. Mason was a good man and Annie wanted to have sex with him. She was going to give him her body by choice, but that didn't mean her heart went along. She wouldn't give that up.

"I'm feeling a serious vibe from your side of the car," he said. "You okay?"

"Better than okay." She was in control.

"We're almost home." His voice was edgy and deep with the subtext of what home would be for them tonight.

A wave of anticipation rolled through her and every nerve ending in her body started to throb. She'd been waiting for this possibly since the first time she'd seen him. Maybe not exactly then because she'd been very tired and pretty crabby. But soon after when he'd kept showing up. That was okay. Falling in love was not.

"Here we are." He drove into the driveway. "Home sweet home."

There was a light on in the living room and the babies weren't there. "Do you think maybe we should call your mom and check on Sarah and Charlie?"

"Yeah." He pulled his cell out of his jeans' pocket and looked at the screen. "There's a text from her."

"What is it?"

"She says, 'Babies fine. Don't call me. I'll call you.'"

"Okay, then. Wow." Annie looked at him. "It's a little scary that she can read minds."

"It's a mom thing. She's one, you're one." He shrugged. "Let's go inside."

"Yeah." She opened her door. "I want to see what the surprise is."

Mason got out and came around to her side. He held out his hand and she put hers into his palm, their fingers intertwining as they walked to the front door and unlocked it.

He pushed it wide and said, "Surprise."

Annie's heart melted when she saw pink rose petals on the entryway floor. The trail continued through the family room and down the hall to the master bedroom. On the dresser was an ice bucket with a bottle of champagne and two flutes.

He lifted the bottle and water rolled off. "The ice is almost melted, but it's still cold."

"Oh, Mason—" She moved closer to him and thought surely he could actually hear her heart hammering. "This is incredibly thoughtful. I didn't think you could top picking me up from work and that beautiful dinner, but I was wrong. You were right. I do thank you."

"Yeah?" He was studying her closely and the words seemed to reassure him. "I'm glad. This could so easily have gone seriously sideways."

"It so didn't, believe me." She put her palms on his chest and met his gaze. "I wasn't tired before, but I'm *really* not tired now."

He grinned sheepishly as his hands settled on her waist and pulled her close. "You're not going to forget that, are you?"

"I think the rose petals and champagne bought you a memory lapse."

"In that case..."

Mason lowered his mouth to hers, a soft kiss, but tension had been building all night. And probably even before that. The touch was like accelerant to a glowing spark, igniting it, turning it into a flame that burned out of control. She opened her mouth and his tongue moved inside, caressing everywhere before dueling with hers.

Annie pushed his sports jacket off his shoulders and he dragged it the rest of the way, turning the sleeves inside out in his rush. She started to undo the buttons on his shirt but her fingers were shaking, her hands uncoordinated. He brushed them aside and dragged it over his head.

Light trickled in from the hallway, enough for her to see the impressive width of his chest and the contour of muscle. It was begging to be touched and Annie couldn't resist. The ever-so-male dusting of hair scraped her palms as she moved them over his skin and down his rib cage. She heard him suck in air and flinch as if it tickled—or turned him on.

"You're very forward," he said.

"I've been told I should take the initiative."

"Do I want to know who told you that?" He picked up her hand and softly caressed the palm with his thumb.

"Probably not."

"Even if I wanted to thank them?" he said in a hoarse voice. "And, just so we're clear, I'm definitely not complaining."

He brought her hand to his mouth and sucked on her index finger. Now it was her turn to gasp as the power of that small contact crackled over the nerve endings in every part of her body. She was breathless and feeling like taking more initiative.

"You have too many clothes on," he said.

"What are you going to do about that?" She gave him a sassy look then unbuckled the belt at his waist.

"I'm going to assist you in disrobing." He turned her around so that her back was to him.

She quickly shrugged off her sweater, making it easier for him to keep his promise. He didn't hesitate, instantly lowering the zipper on the black dress. He did it slowly, and only to her waist, then he pushed the material open wider and kissed the exposed skin.

This exquisite torture was making Annie squirm with need in the best possible way. He must have read her body language because with one quick move he had the zipper all the way down. She let the silky black material slide down her body and pool at her feet before stepping out of it.

She faced him in black panties, matching bra and high heels. He wasn't the only one who could read body language. If the intensity in his eyes was anything to go by, he very much liked what he saw.

"You are so beautiful." His voice was hardly more than a strangled whisper.

He put his hands on her waist, grazing his thumbs over the sensitive bare skin before sliding them higher to brush the undersides of her breasts.

The need to feel his hands on her without any material in the way was so strong she couldn't fight it even if she wanted to. She reached behind and unhooked her bra, letting it fall to the floor with the rest of her clothes. Then she took his hands and placed them on her breasts, holding them there. The touch felt so good, her eyes drifted closed, letting her just take in the sensations.

Moments later she felt his mouth on her and the sensations multiplied exponentially. He kissed first one sensitive peak then the other and her legs went so weak she wasn't sure they would hold her up.

"I want you now," she murmured.

"Twist my arm."

He yanked the bedcovers down then removed the rest of his clothes. Annie stepped out of her heels and let him lead her to their bed. She sat then slid over and made room for him. He followed her, gathered her in his arms and slid his hand over her side to the waistband of her panties. He hooked a thumb then dragged them over her thighs and calves, where she kicked them off.

He ran his hand down her hip and over her belly, resting his palm there as he slid one finger inside her. He brushed his thumb over the sensitive feminine bundle of nerves between her thighs and the intense feeling nearly made her jump off the bed.

All the while he was kissing her—eyelids, nose, cheeks, mouth, neck. He kissed the underside of her jaw then blew softly on the moistness, making her shiver before taking her earlobe between his teeth, biting gently, tenderly. The assault on her senses pushed her to the edge.

"I need you. Now—"

Without a word, he nudged her legs apart with his knee and settled himself over her. His chest was going up and down very fast and the sound of their mingled harsh breaths filled the room. Taking his weight on his forearms, he started to push inside her then stopped.

"What?" she asked.

"A condom—"

"Oh, God! I wasn't thinking—"

"I was." He rolled sideways, reached into the nightstand to retrieve one then put it on. Moments later he was back and kissed her softly. "All squared away. Now, where were we? Oh, yes—"

He entered and her body closed around him, welcoming him. She wrapped her legs around his waist, taking him deeper inside, moving her hips. He got the message and slowly stroked in and out, building the tension with each thrust.

Before she was ready, Annie felt herself let go, break apart, setting free waves of pleasure inside her. Aftershocks made her tremble in the most wonderful way and he held her until they stopped.

Then he began to move in and out again. One thrust then two. Moments later he groaned and breathed her name. She kissed his neck and chest and when he buried his face against her hair, she held him until he sighed into her shoulder.

Annie wasn't sure how long they stayed like that and didn't much care. She hadn't felt this good in a very long time, and that kind of scared her. Sex with Mason was different. Oh, the mechanics were the same, but it was unlike anything she'd ever experienced. And there was only one reason for that.

Her feelings were engaged. She wasn't putting any label on them, but something was stirred up inside her. It was ironic that she'd been bothered when he wouldn't sleep with her. And there was that old saying—be careful what you wish for.

Well, she got it. And she wasn't complaining. It was everything she'd hoped for and more. Mason played her body like a violin and her body was happy. But her heart was a different story.

Chapter Thirteen

Annie didn't trust perfect.

She'd grown up in an environment that was the exact opposite of perfect. The absence of crisis was the bar she used to judge the quality of her life. A rainbows-and-unicorns existence made her uneasy but that's how it had been for the last week. Ever since that magical night when Mason had surprised her at work and taken her to dinner, followed by the best sex she'd ever had.

And it wasn't an aberration because it had happened every night after. Even with babies and work, they managed to be together. It was wonderful but Annie was so afraid to go all in and believe this was how things were going to be from now on. She was a little less confident about her control where Mason was concerned.

He would laugh if she confessed her fears, but he couldn't understand. Except for that one bad marriage blip, his life had been smooth sailing because he'd won the lottery in terms of fabulous families. She couldn't relate to that, so it was understandable that he had no frame of reference for her insecurity, either.

Today her insecurities were on parade inside her. They were meeting his lawyer and the family court judge to finalize his legal petition of paternal rights. He was with Charlie in the family room waiting for her to get Sarah ready.

She smiled at the little girl on the changing table, playing with a small stuffed bear as Annie secured the tabs on her diaper. "Daddy is your daddy, right? So what could go wrong, baby girl?"

Sarah babbled an incoherent response. "I know. I'm being ridiculous. Daddy would say the same thing. It's just that I'm nervous. And you need to look your best. So Mommy has to put your clothes on. No flashing the judge, baby girl."

She slid white tights over Sarah's feet and legs, then covered the diaper. After sitting the infant up, she slipped a dress over her head, a simple floral print with a smocked bodice, and black ballerina flats. Last, she put on a headband with attached bow that highlighted her cornflower blue eyes and blond curls. For once, the little girl didn't pull it off. And again the perception of perfection reared its ugly head.

"I have a bad feeling about this."

She sighed then picked up the baby and walked into the family room. Mason had Charlie in his arms, holding the little boy closer and more tightly than usual. He was wearing navy slacks and a long-sleeved white dress shirt with a red-and-blue-striped silk tie. There was a serious expression on his face and her stomach knots pulled tighter.

"You're worried," Annie said.

"About?"

"Court."

"Nervous," he clarified. "There's a difference. Unless you work there, no one wants to go in front of a judge."

"But your lawyer said it's just a formality. All the paperwork is in order."

"He did," Mason confirmed. "So smile, Annie."

"You first," she challenged.

At that moment Charlie babbled something that sounded like "Da-da" and patted Mason's shoulder with his chubby little hand. And that got a genuine smile from his father.

"See? Charlie isn't worried," Annie said.

"Only about getting his next bottle." Mason tested the weight of the boy resting on his forearm. "Have you noticed how heavy he's getting?"

"I have." She nuzzled her daughter's soft cheek. "This little princess is petite and delicate."

"She looks beautiful. And so do you." For a moment his eyes glittered with something other than anxiety. "Is that a new dress?"

She looked down at the belted black shirtdress with its long sleeves and white detailing. Her coordinating heels were low and sensible. Practical but not flashy. For the moment, anyway, she was living a rainbows-and-unicorns life, so why not dress the part?

"Yes, and new shoes." She caught her bottom lip between her teeth. "Do we look like we're trying too hard?"

"Maybe. But justice is supposed to be blind. I doubt the judge will turn down my petition because of our fashion choices."

"So, you're saying I'm being ridiculous?"

He smiled. "Those words did not come out of my mouth."

"Uh-huh." She looked at Sarah. "See? I told you Daddy would call me silly."

He moved close enough for her to feel the warmth of his body and hers responded to it. Smiling tenderly, he said, "You are the least silly person I know. If anything, I'd like to see you develop a silly streak and work on cultivating a little carefree-ness."

"So now I'm too serious?" she teased.

"You're perfect."

"Not even close." And of all the things he could have said, that was the least likely to anesthetize her nerves. Because she didn't trust perfect.

"That's my prognosis and I'm sticking to it." He shrugged. "But we're procrastinating and need to get going. No one will care how photo ready wc are if we miss the hearing."

"Right."

They shifted into high gear, working together like a meticulously choreographed ballet. Each put a baby into a carrier then took it to the car and secured it in the rear passenger seat. Annie had packed the diaper bag with bottles, changes of clothes and supplies for any emergency imaginable and set it on the floor in front of Charlie. Mason lifted the double stroller into the SUV cargo area. He'd put on his matching suit jacket and looked like a successful doctor and devoted dad.

Annie smiled at him. "You look very handsome. And pretty soon this will all be over."

"Piece of cake." He kissed her, a brief brush of his mouth on hers. "We got this."

They drove to the courthouse located in an older section of Huntington Hills. It was a complex of buildings and Mason's lawyer met them in the lobby of the family court. The high ceilings made their footsteps echo on the marble floor and the twins noticed. Both of them found their outdoor voices and used them in different pitches that made Annie and Mason wince.

She had just met the attorney and wanted their babies

to make a good impression. Like that really mattered, but… "Sorry about that."

Cole Brinkman didn't seem perturbed by the noise. "This is normal for family court. They're kids and no one expects them not to make a sound."

"So this won't count against us?" Mason asked.

"Of course not," the lawyer said. "Nothing will. Through no fault of yours, you didn't know about them. Now you do and have the science to back up your claim. It's a slam dunk."

"Okay." Mason nodded.

"Just so you're aware, there are other cases in front of this judge, too. There will be other parents."

"And kids?" Annie asked.

"Yeah." Cole grinned. "It's going to be noisy."

"Okay, then."

"We should go in. Judge Downey is hearing the case and his courtroom is at the end of the hall."

They walked in the direction he pointed and stopped at the tall, wooden double doors. Mason pulled one open so Annie could push the twins' stroller through. Cole wasn't lying. By Annie's count, there were about eight or ten couples already seated with numerous children of varying ages.

Minutes after they settled in the first row, an older man came in from a side door near the high bench. Since he had on a black robe, one assumed he was the judge. A woman in a sheriff's uniform announced Judge Downey, a man with white hair who looked to be somewhere in his sixties.

"Good morning," he said. "I've reviewed the documents for all of you here today and we'll try to move things along quickly. Children have a short attention span and I want them to go be kids. So, first case."

It wasn't them. From what Annie could pick up, the couple were aunt and uncle to a boy whose parents had been arrested during a drug sting and sent to prison for illegal distribution. The child was born while the mom was in jail and family had petitioned for temporary guardianship of the infant. They were the only parents he'd ever known. Now they were seeking legal custody. Their home environment was stable and loving, but the court bent over backward to keep children with their biological parents unless that became impossible. It was complicated.

Thank goodness Mason's case was simple, Annie thought. Several more couples and kids were called up, but Charlie was getting restless in the stroller so she unbuckled him and set him on her lap. Sarah wouldn't stand for being strapped in if her brother got to be free. So Annie handed off the boy to Mason and released the little girl, holding her close for a moment.

As proceedings dragged on she pulled out bottles from the diaper bag, then toys to entertain them. That worked for a while but then they started rubbing their eyes. After that there were tired cries and she wasn't sure if it was permissible to get up and move around with them. Mercifully their case was called and they could at least walk as far as the judge's bench.

He smiled. "You have a beautiful family, Dr. Blackburne."

"Thank you. I think so, too." He patted Charlie's back.

"A lot of scenarios present in my court, most of them heartbreaking. And I have to make decisions that are in the best interest of a child, decisions that will affect people's lives forever. And not always in a good way."

Annie's stomach lurched. Was he trying to prepare them for the worst? Something no one could have predicted?

Judge Downey smiled then. "Fortunately your situation is not one of those and the facts speak for themselves. Black-and-white. The DNA results are proof that you are the biological father of Charles and Sarah Campbell. They are a conclusive determination of your paternal rights, which I'm pleased to legally affirm."

"Thank you, sir," Mason said.

"Your attorney also filed a concurrent petition to change their last names and that is granted, too."

"So, that's it?" For a second Annie wasn't sure she'd said that out loud.

The judge smiled. "That's it. I wish every case was this easy. Congratulations."

"Thank you, Your Honor." Mason grinned at her, obviously relieved.

They left the courtroom and shook hands with their attorney. Cole took cell phone pictures of them, their first as a legal family.

They left the building and found the SUV. Mason grinned. "We're all Blackburnes now."

"I know." She had been ridiculous to worry.

This was surreal and so wonderful that there were no words to express her feelings. The last piece had fallen into place and she could hardly take it in. She finally had everything she'd ever dreamed of. A traditional family. She had never really believed that happiness like this could happen to someone who'd come from where she had. But she'd beaten the odds.

On paper and in reality her life really was perfect.

Mason drove his family home from the Huntington Hills' government center but he couldn't be sure he wasn't flying. Since getting the DNA results, he'd been there for the babies. He'd fed them, changed diapers, walked the floor at night with either—or both—when necessary. He'd been doing all the right things because he loved them. But there was something profoundly powerful in knowing the t's were crossed and the i's dotted. His status was legal. His name was on their birth certificate. No one could take them away from him.

"I'm pretty happy right now," he said.

"Really?" Annie was in the front passenger seat beside him. "I'd never have guessed. What with you frowning since we left the courtroom."

"I haven't stopped smiling." He was stating the obvious, which she already knew. "It's the weirdest thing. The proof was in the DNA test but I feel as if a weight has been lifted."

"That's good, because you're stuck with me and the twins now, Dr. Blackburne."

"And I can't think of anyone I'd rather share this with."

There was a smile in her voice when she said, "What a sweet thing to say. I feel the same way."

He glanced over and thought again what a pretty picture she made in her new dress. He also thought how very much he was looking forward to getting her out of it. But that was for later. Right now they had to get the kids home for naps. How ordinary that sounded and how wonderful. He vowed never to take it for granted. This was something he'd wanted for a very long time.

Annie seemed happy, too. They'd worked out the sex misunderstanding and were as compatible in bed as they were out of it. She wasn't demanding declarations of love or a definition of his feelings, and he was grateful for that. He cared about her more than he wanted to put into words. A couple of times leaving the house or on the phone when he'd said goodbye and nearly added "I love you," it startled him. But he caught himself. What they had was pretty damn good.

He wasn't going to rock the boat with a four-letter word. He'd said it all the time to his ex, even at the end when he wasn't feeling it anymore. He didn't want anything to mess up what he had with Annie and the kids, especially that one little word.

"We're almost home," he said. Another four-letter word that felt different from when he'd left this morning. Now it was his turn to be silly and Annie would probably make fun of him, but right now he didn't care. "The meaning of home feels more profound to me."

"Like you got a blessing from the angels?"

"At the risk of you laughing at me," he said, "yes."

"I understand." And she wasn't laughing.

He pulled the SUV into the driveway and turned off the engine. "Would it be too corny to say this is the first day of the rest of our lives?"

"Probably. But I get where you're coming from and share the sentiment. Who'd have guessed the big, bad, army doctor, emergency specialist was such a super softy?"

"That's our secret," he said teasingly. "I have a badass reputation to maintain." Belying his words, he took her hand, bringing it to his lips to kiss the back of it. "Let's go be a family."

She glanced into the back seat and smiled tenderly at the sleeping babies. "Car ride works every time."

"Any chance of getting them in their cribs without waking them up?"

"There's always a chance." But the skeptical note in her voice put the brakes on hope. "The odds aren't good."

"That's what I figured. I'll take Sarah and the diaper bag. You get Charlie." He felt as if he was the commander of a military operation, and life with twins was like that sometimes. Double the work. But he wouldn't change it for anything.

"Sounds like a plan."

Coordinating their efforts, they swiftly and efficiently and—dare he say it?—expertly got their children inside and changed out of their perfect family court clothes. One-piece terry-cloth sleepers were just what the doctor ordered. Each of the babies got a bottle and went down for a nap with a minimum of protest. The magic was still holding.

He and Annie tiptoed from the nurseries into the family room and he smiled at her. "That was too easy. Do you think it's because I'm now legally their father as well as biologically?"

"They're just tired out from a big day," she said. "Or maybe we've banked some good karma."

"Since all is quiet on the home front, would you mind if I went out to do an errand?"

"What do you need to do?"

He grinned. "It's a surprise."

"Oh?" Female appreciation turned her eyes a darker shade of hazel, highlighting the gold flecks. "Maybe champagne and rose petals?"

"You're half-right. We need a really good bottle of champagne to celebrate a really good day."

"But no flowers?" She didn't look the least bit disappointed. "It was a sweet and beautiful gesture that I'll never forget. But those petals were really messy. Until they dried, it was kind of hard to vacuum them up. I watched you struggle with that."

"So the whole thing was wasted on you." He knew better than that.

"Absolutely not." She met his gaze and there was a wicked gleam in hers. "But it's not necessary today."

"Good. Because that's not my plan. I wanted to stop by my mom's and share our good news."

"You definitely should. Flo needs to know," she said emphatically. "I have a little work to do anyway. While the kids are sleeping."

"Okay, then. I shouldn't.be too long."

"Take your time."

He nodded and started to turn away, then impulse took over. Moving close, he curved his fingers around her upper arms and pulled her to him, then lowered his mouth to hers. Her body went soft and yielding, and her small sigh of satisfaction made him hot all over. He ran his fingers through her silky blond hair then cupped her cheek in his palm. Her breath caught and she slid her arms around his neck. When he reluctantly lifted his mouth from hers, both of them were breathing hard.

"Are you sure you need to work?" His voice was hoarse.

"Yes. Sorry." And she did look let down. "Bob is doing the presentation to the client tomorrow and I need to go over the sketches and theme one more time, just to make sure it's as perfect as possible."

"Okay. And I really should share our good news."

"Yes."

"'Bye, Annie. I—" He'd almost said it again but stopped just in time. And he wasn't sure how he felt about that.

"What?"

"I'll be back soon. But if you need anything, call the cell."

Mason hurried off and drove to his folks' house not far away. His dad wouldn't be home from work yet but his mom's job was part-time and her car was in the driveway when he got there. He exited the SUV then walked up to the front door and knocked.

Flo answered and smiled instantly when she recognized him. "Mason! This is an unexpected surprise."

"Good or bad?"

She playfully swatted his arm. "Always good to see you. And you know that. Come in."

"Thanks."

"Can I get you something? Iced tea? Coffee? Food?"

"Come to think of it, I'm starving. Didn't have lunch today."

"I'll make you something."

In the kitchen she got out what she needed for a sandwich, even putting on one of the dill pickle slices that he liked. He sat in one of the bar chairs at the island and grabbed the plate she slid over to him.

"Thanks, Mom."

"You're welcome." She walked around the counter and sat in the chair beside his, watching wide-eyed as he wolfed down the food. "Why no lunch? Were you at the hospital? I didn't think you were working today."

"I'm not. But it was a big day. Annie and I went to court with the twins."

"That was today?" Her mouth dropped open and then she gave him the "mom" look. "Why didn't you tell me? I'd have been there."

"That's why we didn't tell you. If something had gone wrong—"

"But your lawyer said there were no problems."

"I just didn't want to take a chance." Now he felt like a little boy caught in a lie. "I know how hard you can take things."

"I admit that, but I'm still pretty good with moral support," she defended. "And you might have needed it. You take things hard, too. Sorry. You got that from me."

"Do you want to keep busting my chops for protecting you? Or do you want to know what happened?"

"Tell me," she said.

He grinned. "It's official. The twins are Charlie and Sarah Blackburne now."

"Oh, Mason." She hugged him. "Congratulations. That's wonderful news."

"It is pretty great."

"And I could have been there to hear it if you'd given me the chance."

"Mom, let it go. I was trying to protect you."

"I'll get over it." She grinned. "I can't wait to tell your dad. Or do you want to talk to him? Since you were obviously trying to protect him, too."

He sighed. "You can tell him. Maybe that will get me off the hook."

"It's a start," she teased.

"Good." He slid off the chair and took his paper plate to the trash. "I have to get back to Annie and the kids. I just wanted to come by and let you know. My next stop before home is for a bottle of champagne."

"You have a lot to celebrate." She hugged him again. "I'm so happy for you, Mason. After all you went through, finally things are going your way."

"Thanks, Mom."

She walked him to the door. "Give my best to Annie and kiss my grandbabies for me. Tell them Grandma will see them soon."

"Will do."

He jogged down the walkway to the SUV parked at the curb and got inside. The next stop was the liquor store and a really expensive bottle of bubbly. He had big plans for it later.

After paying, he got back in the SUV, more than ready to be home with his family.

His cell phone rang and he answered right away, certain it was Annie wanting him to pick up diapers or formula or something. But it wasn't.

"Dr. Blackburne?"

"Yes. Who's this?"

"I'm calling from the lab about the DNA sample you recently had tested."

This was weird. "What about it?"

There was a brief silence before the woman said, "I'm sorry to inform you that the results were incorrect. Recent court action on your motion to claim your parental rights triggered a quality control test here at our company. It turned out there was a mix-up with your sample and the one we received at the same time."

Mason listened to everything the woman said and asked a few questions. He was assured that the tests had been checked and rechecked and the new results were correct. After clicking off the phone, he had no idea how long he sat there. And just like that his world blew up.

"I'm not a father."

Chapter Fourteen

Annie looked at the cell phone in her hand as if it was an alien being. The message from the lab came completely out of the blue and the worst part was that Mason had received the same one. The lab had mixed up the two samples she'd sent. The man who'd signed away his rights to the twins was a DNA match to them. Not Mason.

She couldn't imagine what he was thinking right now. Being a father was so important to him. In fact his first marriage had imploded because his wife had given up on them. Annie didn't quit. She wasn't like that. He would be home soon and they'd talk this through. She would assure him that everything was fine.

But time passed and he didn't come home. She called and he didn't pick up. She left voice messages and he didn't answer. He'd gone radio silent. Once she'd come very close to contacting his parents but decided against it. They would have to know soon, but he should be the one to break that news.

The twins woke up hungry so she fed them then did baths and playtime before getting them down for the night without much fuss. They were obviously still tired from their court outing. It had been several hours and still no Mason.

Another sixty minutes went by. She knew because she counted every one of them. If she didn't hear from him soon, she would find out if his parents had. Worry wasn't something she handled especially stoically.

She was pacing and just about to call Flo when the front door opened. Relief washed over her when he came into the kitchen.

"Mason—"

She moved toward him then saw despair on his face and stopped. He was still wearing his suit but the slacks and jacket were wrinkled, the tie loosened. The crisply pressed-and-perfect exterior was gone and seemed to reflect his inner turmoil.

"Where have you been?" she asked.

"Driving."

"You heard from the lab." She wasn't asking a question.

"I did." He set a bottle of champagne on the granite countertop beside him. A bottle that would probably never be opened. "Turns out we didn't have to get married after all."

The words were like an arrow to her heart and she nearly gasped. She didn't know what she'd expected, but that wasn't it.

"The reasons we got married are still the same."

"What were they again?" His voice was flat, emotionless and just this side of bitter.

"You wanted a family and so did I. Now we have one," she said.

"You do." He dragged his fingers through his hair. "You're their aunt. A blood relative, at least. I, on the other hand, am nothing to them."

"That's not true, Mason. You are Sarah and Charlie's dad. A test done in a lab doesn't change that."

"You're wrong. It changes everything."

"All it means is you probably can't donate bone marrow or a kidney. In every other way you are what you've always been. The man who holds them when they cry. Feeds them when they're hungry. Makes sure their diapers are changed. You keep them safe. Everything a father is supposed to do."

"Annie, it's not that simple."

"It's exactly that simple. You feel the same way about them that you did this morning when you were nervous about what was going to happen in court."

"Yeah." He laughed but the sound was cynical, resentful, frustrated. "The timing of this news is inconvenient. Makes you wonder if fate is having a laugh at our expense."

"What does that mean?"

"I have to notify my attorney about this. It's not as straightforward as it was this morning. The judge should have this information."

"Probably. But I don't think it alters anything. The biological father already signed away his rights. He doesn't want them."

"He did that before test results were in. Knowing for sure gives you a different perspective. Trust me on that."

Annie looked into his eyes, dark with anger and pain. She prayed for the right words to get through to him. "Tell me you don't love them. In spite of this glitch. I want to hear you say that you don't want to be their father."

"I—" He looked down and shook his head. "That's not the issue."

"Are you serious? It's exactly the issue, the only thing that matters."

"I'm nothing to them." He slashed his hand through the air as if severing ties. "I was something for a while. For a few months I had a son and a daughter. For a few weeks I had it all. Test results matter or we wouldn't do them."

"In a medical situation they do, obviously. But it isn't relative to the heart and soul."

"Relative?" His smile was sarcastic. "Are you making a pun?"

"Stop feeling sorry for yourself, Mason." She took a step closer and realized how badly she wanted him to hold her and to hold him back. "They are your children in every way that counts. And they need you."

"I've lost my children. Again." Rage and hurt blazed in his eyes before they went dark. "And there's nothing I can do about it."

"Let's take a time-out." Annie met his gaze. "This has been a shock for both of us. We need to let the dust settle and let it wear off. Deep breath. Decisions should wait until we've processed this completely."

"It's not complicated, Annie. Time and cooler heads won't change the fact that the twins are not mine."

It wasn't the words so much as the look in his eyes that convinced Annie his mind was made up. Nothing she could say would sway him. "Wow, you're not the man I thought."

"What does that mean?"

"I believed you were someone who didn't put restrictions on love. It never occurred to me that you are a man who can't care about a child unless that child has his genetic material."

"That's not fair," he said.

"I think it is," she snapped. "And what about you and me? What happened to sharing this adventure together? You said that to me just today, but I'm getting a totally different vibe now. The fact is that we're married and we have two children."

"You do," he corrected.

"Back to that." She blew out a breath. He was hurt and betrayed and too big for her to shake some sense into him. "So where does that leave us?"

He opened his mouth then closed it again. But emotions were swirling in his eyes: pain, bitterness, betrayal because of a stupid mistake, regret. And that was the one tearing her apart. He was sorry he married her.

Annie hated being right. Mason Blackburne was one more man abandoning her. She should have been prepared for the fact that sooner or later he would back away. Unfortunately she wasn't. She had let down her guard and got a right hook square in the heart.

"Message received," she said. "This is your house. I'll move out, but I'd appreciate a little time to find something for the babies and me."

"Annie, we—"

She put up a hand to stop him. "You made it clear there is no we, so it's a little late to play that card. Until I can move out, I'm taking the master bedroom. I'd appreciate it if you'd sleep in the guest room."

"If that's what you want."

No, it's not what she wanted, but it was the only choice he was giving her. This wasn't a misunderstanding about whether or not they would assume traditional husband and wife roles and have sex. He'd all but told her that since his DNA didn't match the twins', he didn't want her.

"Good night, Mason."

Without a backward look, Annie walked away and down the hall. She went into the room she'd so happily shared with Mason and closed the door to shut him out.

She'd been clueless and overconfident believing she was in control of her feelings. Now she knew that what she felt for Mason was too big to contain. She was head over heels in love with him and knew it for a fact. Because letting him go was so much harder than any rejection she'd ever experienced in her life.

He'd only married her to do the right thing for the children he'd believed were his. It was clear to her now that she would never have married him if she hadn't been in love with him. The worst part was she couldn't even blame him. She'd agreed to everything he'd proposed.

She tried to hold back the sobs, but one escaped before she put her hands over her mouth. Mason had broken her heart but she would never let him know how much he'd hurt her.

Mason was a mess.

That was his diagnosis and there wasn't any medication or therapy that would make him better. It had been a few days since finding out he wasn't a father and he still felt as if someone had cut out his heart and left a gaping hole where it used to be. He and Annie had been unfailingly polite when forced to interact, but every night he heard her crying and it ripped him apart. So he'd decided to do something proactive.

He'd gotten in touch with the twins' biological father. Annie had his contact information in a file, along with paperwork relinquishing all rights to them. Mason wasn't their blood relative but Tyler Sherman was. And kids needed a dad. The guy reluctantly agreed to meet him during his lunch break and suggested neutral territory. Patrick's Place.

Mason had pushed back on the location because it had memories, but the man insisted. It wasn't far from his current landscape job. Apparently he wasn't inclined to go out of his way for his children.

So Mason was waiting in a booth. He glanced around the place where he and Annie had taken vows not so long ago. The bar with brass foot rail dominated the room and there were personal family photos of the owners on the wall behind it. A room adjacent to this one had pool tables, flat-screen TVs mounted on the wall and comfortable seating to watch televised sporting events. Next to that was the restaurant where they'd had dinner with his family after the wedding. The tables were nearly full during the lunch hour. Coming here was a really bad idea.

So he turned away and focused on the front door, where he could see everyone who came in. There were couples, groups of women and men, even lone individuals who'd stopped by for something to eat. But no one who seemed to be looking for someone. The meet time came and went and he was beginning to think he'd been stood up until he saw a guy enter by himself then hesitate and look around.

"Tyler?" Mason said quietly.

"Yeah." He was tall, blond and really young. Dressed in jeans and a navy T-shirt with Sherman Landscape silkscreened on the front.

"Mason Blackburne." He stood and held out his hand.

The other man shook it then sat across from him. He looked acutely uncomfortable. "What's this about? You insisted it was important. You said it was about the DNA test."

"Yeah, you are the twins' father." Mason was surprised those words didn't stick in his throat. A lab test didn't change his love for those babies and that meant he wanted them to have everything they deserved.

"Is this some kind of scam? Annie said the DNA would be done in five business days. That was months ago. Why are you telling me this now?"

Mason swallowed hard. "The lab made a mistake and

we just found out about it. They mixed up the samples—yours and mine."

Tyler looked down at his hands for a moment then blew out a long breath. "I signed a legal document giving Annie sole custody."

"That was before you knew for sure that you're their father. You might change your mind." Mason pulled out his cell phone and found the pictures he'd taken right after court, the day he'd claimed parental rights he wasn't entitled to. "Here they are."

Tyler scrolled through the series of photographs but his expression didn't change. "They look healthy. Cute kids. Look like Annie."

"Yeah."

He handed back the phone. "But why would you think I'd change my mind?"

"I just found out that the babies I thought were mine are actually not. I won't lie. This information hit me pretty hard because I've wanted to be a dad very badly and for a long time. It seemed to me that the man who is their biological father would jump at the chance to claim Charlie and Sarah."

"Does Annie know you contacted me?"

"I didn't want to say anything until after I talked to you. But these kids deserve to know their real father." Since he felt like their real father, it tore him up to even say that.

"Look, I'm not father material and maybe I never will be. My childhood was crap and my old man was a son of a bitch, probably still is. I wouldn't know because I refuse to see him. The fact is I doubt I'd be a very good father because my role model sucked."

Mason had always taken his close family life for granted, until he'd met Annie. She'd told him more than once how lucky he was to have his parents and siblings, and this guy was confirming that.

Mason met the other man's gaze. "So you're sure about this? The decision is right for you?"

"Some choices are hard, but this isn't one of them. Especially because they have Annie and you." He shoved his fingers through his blond hair. "Look, I'm not a complete bastard. If there's a health issue, or someday they're curious about me, I'll do what's right. But as far as raising them? Those kids are better off without me."

"Okay."

Tyler looked at his linked fingers for a moment then back up. "I know what you're thinking."

"I doubt that." Mason almost laughed. There's no way he could possibly know.

"It's nothing I haven't thought about. I should have been more responsible about birth control if I feel so strongly about not having kids."

"Now that you mention it…"

"Believe it or not, I'm very conscientious about that. I wore a condom. It broke, but I didn't think too much about it because Jessica told me she was on the Pill. Those twins were meant to be, I guess."

"Apparently."

"Look, Dr. Blackburne, I made the right call—for me and for them. You obviously care and they're lucky to have you. If it matters, you have my blessing."

Oddly enough, it did matter. "Thanks for not blowing off this meeting, Tyler."

"You're welcome." He slid out of the booth and held out his hand. "Nice to meet you."

"Same here." Mason stood and shook his hand then watched the man exit the way he'd come.

"You look like someone who needs a drink." The voice came from behind him, but it was familiar.

Mason had been so lost in his own thoughts, he hadn't heard anyone approach. He turned and saw Leo "The Wall" Wallace, a former NHL star who co-owned this place with his wife.

"Hi, Leo."

"How are Annie and the kids?"

"Healthy." Physically, anyway. She would barely look at him and cried every night, so there was that.

The big man was studying him intently. "Well, my friend, you look like hell."

"Since when did insulting a customer become a good marketing strategy?" No matter how true it might be.

"It's just an observation and I wasn't kidding about that drink. Have a seat. I'll be right back."

"It's too early," Mason protested.

"You're the doctor but you don't always know what's best."

Mason did as instructed and watched the other man walk over to the bar and say something to the bartender. Instantly the woman got two glasses then took a bottle of some kind of brown liquor from the display behind the bar. She poured, then slid the tumblers across the bar to her boss. Leo carried them to the table, setting one in front of Mason.

"Drink up, Doc. It's medicinal."

Mason looked at it for a moment then, figuring he couldn't feel any worse, he tossed back the contents of his glass. It was smooth going down then burned in his chest and all the way to his gut. At least for a few moments the searing sensation took his mind off the pain eating up his insides.

Leo toyed with his glass. "So, who was that guy you were talking to? The conversation looked pretty intense."

Mason saw no reason not to tell him. His family knew and had tried to help. But what could they say? Words didn't change the results of the test. Talking this through might help. Although he wasn't sure how. It wouldn't change the fact that the rug had been ripped out from under him and the truth he thought he knew was a lie.

"That guy I talked to is the twins' biological father." He explained about the lab error.

"I'm speechless." Leo looked like he'd just been smacked with a hockey stick. Finally he said, "How is Annie taking this?"

"Better than me. She says it doesn't make any difference. Love is all that matters."

The other man's expression turned dark and serious. "She's right."

"Wait a minute. You're a guy. I thought you'd understand."

"You mean take your side. And I do understand. More than you think." Leo tossed back the liquor in front of him then toyed with the glass. "I was married once before. We had a baby boy and I love him more than I can say."

"Okay. Didn't know that, but I'm not sure what this has to do with my situation."

"He's not mine biologically. She lied to me, said she was pregnant with my child, and I married her. After a couple of years when she was having an affair with the guy, she said her son should be raised by his *real* father."

Pain darkened the man's eyes and he sucked in a breath. "The thing is, I felt like his real father. I changed diapers, fed him, played with him, got up at night when he cried. Loved him more than anything. It doesn't get more real than that, but suddenly I had no say in any decisions con-

cerning my son, simply because he didn't have my DNA."
Leo met his gaze. "Everything changed except the way
I felt about him."

"Oh, man—" Mason shook his head. "Now I don't
know what to say."

"Tess and I got off to a rocky start emotionally, but
there was this irresistible physical attraction from the moment we met. One night we gave in to it and she got pregnant. She swore the baby was mine, but I'd been burned
once and didn't want to be made a fool of again. It nearly
ruined the best thing that ever happened to me."

"That's rough."

"Yeah. But now the most wonderful woman in the
world is mine and we have a beautiful little girl." His expression brightened. "My point in telling you this is that I
have a pretty good idea what you're going through. And I
have to say that meeting with the twins' biological father
seems straight up to me."

"I appreciate that." Mason remembered his conversation with Annie the night he'd found out about the error. It
was bitter and full of self-pity. "But Annie... I said some
things."

"People say stupid stuff when they're dealing with really emotional situations. It's understandable."

"Not this."

Leo frowned. "What did you say to her?"

"That we didn't need to get married."

"I'm sorry... What?"

Mason sighed. "I told her—"

"I heard what you said." His friend stared at him as if
he had two heads. "You implied that you only married
her because you believed you were the twins' father?"

Mason winced. "When you say it like that—"

"I'm guessing that she wasn't happy."

"She's moving out with the kids as soon as she can find a place to live," he confirmed.

"You are an outstanding doctor, but communication is not really your thing." Leo gave him a pitying look. "So, genius, why *did* you marry Annie?"

Mason was running on pure adrenaline now and just snapped out the answer without overthinking it. "I'm in love with her and the babies. I love her so much that I'll let her go if that's what's best for them. Even if it kills me."

And just saying those words, he died a little more. But he meant it.

"You're a damn fool, Mason."

"What?"

"This isn't some romantic tragedy. This is real life. You have a beautiful woman who loves you." Leo pointed a finger at him. "Don't give me that look. I know what I'm talking about. You may not believe this, but I'm a lot more than just an ex-jock businessman. I saw the way she was looking at you the night you got married. Right here at Patrick's Place. Trust me. Those were not the looks of a woman getting married just for the sake of the kids."

They had deliberately avoided defining anything besides friendship and respect—even in their wedding vows. And what Mason felt was so much more than that or he never would have proposed in the first place.

"Oh, man… I really blew it," Mason said.

"You think?" Leo pointed at him again. "You gotta fix this, pal. And trust me. It won't be easy."

He was right, Mason thought. He had to fix things with Annie. But how?

Chapter Fifteen

"Bob wants to see you in his office."

Annie was working in her cubicle and looked over her shoulder at Ella, who was standing right outside. "What does he want?"

"Don't know. He just told me to tell you. Consider yourself told."

"Did he look happy? Sad? Mad?"

Ella thought about the question. "Not sure. If people's faces were emojis, I could tell you."

"Point taken. And it has to be said, no one can tell what Bob is feeling. He's remarkably even-tempered."

"He is." Ella studied her. "You, on the other hand, wear your heart on your sleeve."

Annie really hoped that wasn't true. Because then everyone would know how crushed she was about why Mason married her. "Really?"

"Are you kidding? Everyone in the office has been wondering what's been bugging you for the last couple of days."

"No way," Annie said. "I'm the same as always."

"That's not what Cruz says, and he's right next door to you."

"What is he saying?"

"That since the night Mason picked you up here and took you to dinner you've been so bright and shiny it makes his head hurt. But the last few days, you look like someone popped your wedded-bliss balloon."

Hmm, she hadn't realized her cubicle buddy was so observant. Or that she was so transparent. Or that she could miss Mason's touch so much it was impossible to hide her feelings about him. Being humiliated in school because of her learning disability had been the training ground for her poker face. Only Jessica had been able to tell when she was concealing her pain and anguish. But apparently now her coworkers could, too.

"I'm fine. Just tired. With two babies in the house, who can sleep?" Duck, cover and conceal.

Old habits died hard and she didn't want to talk about this. The babies had been sleeping better than those first few months after she'd brought them home from the hospital. It was Mason keeping her up. All the what-ifs and if-onlys haunted her. How could she have been stupid enough to fall for him? That was actually the easiest question to answer.

Chemistry. She'd felt it from the beginning and it wasn't something easily ignored. Plus he was so darn nice, a truly good man. Practically perfect, which was ironic because she didn't trust perfect. Yet she'd started to trust him and her heart hadn't stood a chance.

"I'm fine, Ella."

"Okay." The woman's tone said she wasn't buying that. "But if you need someone to talk to, I'm here."

"Thanks." She pushed the chair away from her desk and stood. "I'll go see what Bob wants."

"Right."

Annie could tell by her coworker's expression that she was hurt and just wanted to help. It was much appreciated, but she was on the emotional edge and desperately clinging to her professionalism at work. And just before a meeting with her boss was not a good time to air out her personal problems.

She walked to his office. The door was open and he was at his desk. "You wanted to see me?"

"Annie. Yes." He took off his glasses and tossed them on the desk. "Come in. Would you close the door, please?"

She did as requested then sat in the chair on the other side of his desk. "Are you firing me? Should I be worried?"

"No." He smiled. "Just the opposite."

"The opposite would be not firing me."

"I'm making the announcement in the morning to the staff, but I wanted to tell you first."

"About?"

"I'm putting you in charge of the campaign for our newest client." Bob's face grew rounder when he smiled broadly.

"We got the account."

"Yes. In no small part because of your talent and hard work."

"It was a team effort," she said.

"A team that you organized and led." He nodded at her. "Congratulations."

"Thank you."

This was a real "how do you like me now" moment to everyone who ever bullied, teased and belittled her. To anyone who'd called her stupid. This was what she'd worked her butt off for. Against the odds and while raising two infants, she'd managed to come up with creative concepts and execute them, enough to impress a major company and get them to trust C&J Graphic Design with their business.

Now she would be in charge of that account. How she wished Jessica could see her now. She should be doing the dance of joy, except none of it meant anything to her because she'd lost Mason and the family they had made together.

To her horror and humiliation, Annie burst into tears. She buried her face in her hands for several moments then pulled herself together with an effort to look at her boss. "Sorry. That wasn't weird at all."

"Not quite the reaction I expected," he admitted.

"Tears of joy. Honestly." She tried to smile but knew it was wobbly at best.

"You should be proud, Annie. It was a lot of pressure and you've handled it with grace, intelligence and enthusiasm."

"Thank you." She brushed away tears that just kept leaking out of her eyes for no reason.

"I think you should take the rest of the day off. You deserve it. Go home. Let off some steam. Be with your beautiful family."

That nearly sent her into another meltdown because that family was gone. But she managed to maintain her composure long enough to thank him again and walk out of his office.

Family. The idea of it got to her every time. It was the opposite of her superpower. It was her vulnerability. For a pathetically short period of time she'd had everything. The babies, a husband and father, in-laws she loved. It was idyllic. Then a lab error had torn her perfect world apart.

She grabbed her purse from her cubicle and managed to sneak out without seeing anyone. She found her car in the parking lot and put the key in the ignition. But where was she going? Mason wasn't working today and had the twins. He'd insisted, but that was probably all about guilt.

He was clear on the fact that he had a legal responsibility to the babies but insisted he wasn't allowed to have an emotional one. With her promotion, she would probably have to spend more time in the office and that meant hiring someone to watch her children. She couldn't count on him. Not anymore.

As badly as she wanted to see Sarah and Charlie, to hold them, she couldn't face Mason in this raw state. So she backed the car out of the space and drove out of the lot. Instead of taking the turn to go to his house, she went in the opposite direction.

For a long time she just kept driving as thoughts tumbled through her mind. She was operating on autopilot, but her subconscious took over. That was the only explanation for how she eventually ended up at Florence Blackburne's house and saw the woman's car parked in the driveway.

Annie made a spontaneous decision to stop. She parked in front, walked up to the door then rang the bell. Flo answered almost right away. She was holding Sarah. In the background Charlie was crying.

"Boy am I glad to see you." The other woman acted as if nothing had changed. "These two are both hungry. I know they can hold their own bottles now, but I prefer to hold them."

"Me, too. But sometimes you can't."

"The downside of being a twin is having to share because there aren't enough adults around to help."

"This isn't one of those times. I'll go get him," Annie said.

Working together, they warmed bottles and settled on the sofa in the family room. Each of them had a baby to feed.

Annie couldn't get the bottle into Charlie's mouth fast enough. But when she did, there was silence as he sucked the formula down. "Where did Mason go? Did the hospital call him in?"

"No. He said he had to see someone and was going to Patrick's Place."

Annie felt a knot in her stomach. "Another woman?"

"If so, I don't think he'd have mentioned that to me," Flo said. Then her expression changed from teasing to concern. "What's going on with you two? He told us about the lab error, Annie. But I'm not sure why your first thought would be about him meeting another woman."

Annie sighed. Her subconscious had brought her there for a reason. Talking to Mason's mother certainly couldn't make things worse than they already were. "He all but told me he only married me because he thought he was the babies' father."

The other woman took the bottle away from Sarah then lifted her up for a burp, and she produced a very unladylike one. Flo rubbed her back and met Annie's gaze. "The truth of finding out he's not their father threw him. Mason is solid and steady, unflappable. But he was rocked by this. And he's a doctor. He relies on lab tests being correct so that he can treat his patients accordingly."

"I get that. He wasn't the only one shocked by it."

"I know, honey. Although it may sound like it, I'm not taking sides. The thing is, when he was married before, having a family was his focus. So many times he got his hopes up, only to be devastated by losing a child. And it was even harder for Christy, his ex." Flo shook her head. "But with Sarah and Charlie, they were here and they were his. And that was a dream come true for him. I don't know what he said to you, but I doubt he was thinking clearly when he said it."

"He said there was no reason to be married."

"Unless you're in love."

When the baby stopped sucking on the bottle, Annie took it away to burp him. "It was a mistake. Gabriel was right. We moved too fast."

"Gabe's experience doesn't make him the best person to be giving out advice. I wouldn't take his words to heart." She smiled at the baby dozing contentedly on her shoulder. "I'm the one who told Mason not to let you get away and implied that your old boyfriend was hovering."

"Why would you do that?"

"Because you're perfect together."

"I don't believe in perfect," Annie said. "And when he proposed, we agreed that love had nothing to do with it."

Flo smiled. "But neither one of you stuck to that, did you?"

"It doesn't matter. I'm moving out of the house with the babies as soon as I can find a place to go."

Mason's mother shook her head. "I can't believe you're really going to split up. Annie, you're part of the family. So are the twins."

"They're not. Now we know you're not related to them by blood. They're not your grandchildren."

"You're wrong about that." Flo's voice was kind and gentle when she said the words. It was also firm. "Sarah and Charlie are my grandchildren and I love them with every fiber of my being. DNA is only science. It cannot tell us who we're supposed to love. That's the heart's job."

"Flo, I can't believe—"

"Believe it," she said. "And I believe with all my heart that Mason loves you with all of his. Don't throw that away because he said something in haste after getting the biggest shock of his life. Fight for your family."

The woman's words were the verbal equivalent of a snap-out-of-it slap. It worked. Annie got the message. Perfect didn't just happen. You had to fight for it.

* * *

Mason left Patrick's Place feeling both empowered and idiotic. The things he'd said to Annie... He needed to see her as soon as possible and headed to his mother's house to pick up Sarah and Charlie. After parking at the curb, he jogged to the front door and knocked softly. Because of Annie, he was aware that when there were babies in the house, ringing the bell put a guy at the top of the most endangered species list.

The door opened and his mom put a finger to her lips and then indicated he should follow her into the family room. "They're asleep."

"I figured. The thing is, I have to get home and—"

"Cool your jets."

"Mom, you don't understand—"

"Baloney. I understand plenty." She gave him a look. "What in the world is wrong with you?"

"That's a broad question. You might want to narrow the scope a bit because there's a lot wrong with me."

"You're so smart in so many ways that it shocks me how you can be so dense about certain things."

"What are you talking about?" he asked.

"I talked to Annie. How could you tell her you didn't have to be married after all?" His mom pointed a warning finger at him. "And don't even accuse her of talking behind your back."

"I wasn't going to—"

"Because I pried the information out of her. She's an amazing young woman and you have handled everything so clumsily."

"Tell me something I don't know."

"This is not a news flash. You really screwed up. I explained how emotionally drained you were after the divorce, but you need to talk to her and work this out."

"I get it—"

"Because Charlie and Sarah *are* my grandbabies and I love them. Annie, too. She's become like a daughter to your father and me—"

When her mouth quivered and tears filled her eyes, Mason felt like toxic waste. What kind of a son was he, making his mother cry? "It's okay—"

"No, it's not. But you're going to sort everything out." She blinked away the tears. "Because ultimately your welfare is on the line. Only you know what's in your heart, but I can say in all honesty that I've never seen you as happy as you've been with Annie and your family."

"I know and—"

"So you have to convince her not to move out. At least encourage her to give it some time, let emotions settle down before making a decision you'll both regret."

"That's my plan. I will—"

"I mean it, Mason. You've always been an overachiever, so if there's ever been a time to go with your strength, this is it—"

"Mom, stop talking. I just came to get the kids. I'm going to talk to Annie when she gets home from work."

"She got off work early and stopped by to talk to me."

"She didn't take the kids home?"

"I suggested she leave them with me so you two can talk quietly and without interruption. And I'm suggesting the same thing to you. Besides, they're sleeping. Everyone knows you never wake a sleeping baby."

"Okay, thanks."

She smiled. "And, Mason?"

"Yeah?"

"You better explain to Annie who your meeting was with at Patrick's Place."

"How does she know about that?"

His mother shrugged. "She asked where you were so I repeated what you told me, which was next to nothing. She went straight to wondering if it was a woman."

"Great. Like I needed another challenge. And no. I didn't see a woman."

"Make sure she knows that."

He planned to. And it was going to be an uphill battle. She'd told Dwayne the Douche that he'd abandoned her once and she wouldn't give him a chance to do it again. For the first time in his life, Mason wished he was a lawyer instead of a doctor. He needed the right words to heal the harm he'd done to her heart.

The drive from his parents' house wasn't long but it felt like forever. People facing death often said their life flashed before their eyes. Mason had the reverse sensation—life without Annie stretched in front of him. The images were sad and grim, without brilliance or color.

He pulled into the driveway beside her compact car and got out. After gathering his thoughts, he exited the SUV and walked to the front door. He opened it and walked inside. It was unnaturally quiet; a preview of his future if he'd irreparably damaged their relationship.

He couldn't stand the silence and called out, "Annie?"

"In the kitchen."

There was too much square footage between them to accurately diagnose her tone. So he took a deep breath and put one foot in front of the other until he was beside the granite-topped island, face-to-face with her.

"Hi."

"Hi." Her expression was neutral and he didn't know how to take that. If things were normal between them, he would ask about her day. But everything was wrong and what he said to her now would determine whether or not he could make them right again.

He jumped straight into the deep end of the pool.

"I didn't meet a woman at Patrick's Place."

"I believe you. But whatever it was must be pretty important if you had to leave the kids with your mom."

"It had everything to do with their future. And ours," he said. "I talked to Tyler Sherman."

"Their biological father." Her eyes went wide with shock. "Why? He made it clear that he didn't want anything to do with them."

"That was before he knew the test results. I thought he had a right to know."

She mulled that over before asking, "And?"

"The new information didn't change his mind." Mason told her everything the guy had said. "If needed, he'll step up, but feels that day to day the kids are better off without him."

Her expression wasn't neutral now. It was full of doubt. "Were you hoping he did want them now, because you're not their biological father?"

"No. God, no, Annie." He was blowing this. Damn it. "I was trying to do what's right. I would die for Charlie and Sarah. I am and will always be their father. I love them more than I can even put into words. And if he sincerely wanted to be a positive part of their lives, it's my responsibility to look at the big picture and do my damnedest to figure out what's best for them."

"So he doesn't want a role in their lives?"

Mason shook his head. "Not now. But he's not hiding, either. If they have questions eventually, he'll be around to answer them."

"Okay. He sounds like a good guy."

"He seems to be. Self-aware and practical. He cares about the twins, enough to put their welfare first. I respect that."

She took one step back. "Okay, if that's all—"

"That's not even close to all." He wanted so much to have her in his arms, but he was afraid to touch her yet. Afraid she would shrug off his touch and not really *hear* him. "I didn't mean what I said, Annie. About being married. It was a knee-jerk reaction to that call from the lab. Nothing changed for me."

"Oh?" Her eyebrow lifted. "So we're still friends who only like and respect each other?"

"No."

"So we don't like each other?"

"That's not what I meant." This was not going at all the way he'd hoped. "More than anything I want to be married to you. I want a family with you, to raise Charlie and Sarah together with you. They're my kids and it's not in the DNA, it's in the heart. I want to be the best husband and father I can possibly be. Because I love you, Annie."

"Really?"

"With everything I've got. If you give me another chance, I'll prove to you that I will never let you down again."

"Right." She turned away then and walked down the hall toward the master bedroom.

Mason stood there for several moments before reaction kicked in. It was not going to end like this. He wasn't going to let it end at all. Whatever he had to do, however long it took, he was going to prove to her that he loved her and wasn't going away. His military training kicked in and surrender wasn't an option. Army strong.

He marched after her into the room they'd shared awkwardly at first and then with all the passion and intimacy of a married couple. He was so focused on what to say that might persuade her to take a risk on him that it was several moments before he really saw the room.

Rose petals had been tossed on the carpet and the bed.

A bottle of champagne was icing in a bucket and two flutes were beside it on the dresser. Best of all—Annie was there smiling at him. She'd set a scene, just like he had, to work out the bumps in their marriage.

"What's this?" he asked.

"My way of fighting for our family."

"It's a good way." He moved close and put his arms around her waist, nestling her against his body. "So, this— the flowers and champagne—is going to be our thing?"

"Could be," she said. "What do you think?"

"Maybe we should invest in a rosebush." He met her gaze and with all the intensity of the feelings inside him said, "I'm in love with you, Annie. More than I can tell you."

"I know." She settled her hands on his chest. "Deep down I knew that when you proposed or I would never have said yes, no matter how much we pushed the friendship angle."

"How could you know when I didn't?"

"It was there in everything you did. Going to work. Feedings in the middle of the night. Walking the floor with a fussy baby." She glanced at the petal-strewn bed. "Making the effort to show me how you felt even when you wouldn't say the words. At night, reaching for me even in your sleep."

"I knew it, too." He pulled her close and whispered against her hair. "Love is also being afraid I'd lost you when you fell down the stairs and broke your leg. I finally know what it means to be in love."

"I love you more." She glanced at the bed again then up at him.

"In case you were wondering," he said, "I'm not the least bit tired."

She grinned. "Me, either."

Epilogue

Mason parked the SUV in front of his parents' house and smiled at Annie in the passenger seat. The outside looked like a Christmas store had thrown up on it. "So it's the twins' first Christmas."

Annie was staring at the house. Flo had invited the whole family to help decorate, but the scope of it all still amazed her. "Something tells me this has nothing to do with our children."

"You would be right about that. My mom goes all out for Christmas. She's missed having little ones to fuss over and has probably set retail records this year."

A feeling of melancholy slipped into her heart. "Jess would have loved this."

Mason reached over and took her hand, wrapping it protectively in his. "And you still miss her."

"I always will." She had Mason now and the twins. They were happy, healthy and beautiful. Marriage to him was the best thing that had ever happened to her. "I wish she was here."

"She is," he said gently. "She will always be here because a part of her lives on in the twins. And she loved them more than anything."

"How do you know?"

"Because she gave them to you. She trusted you with what she cared about most. And you are honoring her memory by raising them to be the best they can be."

She loved the love shining in his eyes for her. "*We* are loving and caring for them."

"And each other."

"Ma—" That earsplitting screech came from the back seat.

Annie winced. "The pitch of our son's voice could shatter glass."

"Doesn't that make you proud?" he asked. "He's not a year old yet and is pulling himself up to a standing position. Before you know it, he'll be walking. Have you seen how fast he can crawl?"

"Seen it?" she scoffed. "I've had to chase him down. And Sarah is no slouch, either. This 'getting around' thing adds a whole new dimension to parenting."

"I know. Are you as tired as I am?"

"You don't look nearly as tired as I feel. How do men do that?" She studied him. "You complain about being old and tired but you, sir, are better-looking and hotter than ever."

There was a wicked gleam in his eyes. "So, I have a plan. My whole family is here for Christmas. We let them chase after Charlie and Sarah and save our energy. When we get home, I'll have my way with you."

She grinned. "Not if I have my way with you first."

When there was a double outcry of frustration at being

immobilized in the back seat, Annie sighed. "I suppose there's no putting it off any longer. We have to set them free."

"Yeah. Here we go."

They exited the SUV and each opened a rear door. While Mason liberated their daughter, Annie released the restraints, lifted Charlie from the car seat and kissed his cheek. "Is that better, Charlie bear?"

The little boy immediately wriggled and squirmed to be let down but she held on. His grandparents had seen him last night in his white shirt, red-and-green-plaid bow tie and little jeans. Sarah had been wearing her red-velvet dress, white tights and black Mary Janes. Pictures had been taken for posterity. Today for the Christmas gathering they were wearing comfortable T-shirts underneath their sweaters.

Annie looked up at Mason and grinned, preparing to hit him with her most recent Daddy observation. "Our daughter has you wrapped around her little finger."

"Does not," he said.

"Does, too."

They grinned at this now familiar debate then walked up to the front door. Of course Charlie wanted to ring the doorbell because one time he'd been allowed to and had never forgotten.

Flo opened the door and instantly smiled at each baby. "Merry Christmas, my little sweethearts!"

Her husband joined her and beamed at his grandchildren. "Who's having their first Christmas at Grandma and Grandpa's house?"

The twins held out their arms to the older couple and, of course, they were swept into loving hugs and kisses. After the affectionate greeting, they all went into the family room, where everyone was gathered.

The *family* room. A place where relatives were together. To celebrate peace on earth and goodwill toward men.

Or just to hang out on a Sunday. Most people took it for granted, but not Annie. She would never get tired of this.

"Did you see that?" Mason asked her.

"What?"

"They didn't say a word to us. Just commandeered our children without acknowledging our presence." He sighed. "It's official."

"What's that?"

"We're chopped liver."

Annie laughed then slid her hand into his as they mingled with his brothers, sister and parents. There was a gorgeous tree in the corner and wrapped presents were piled underneath it. Lighted garland draped the fireplace mantel, where stockings for every family member were filled to overflowing. It was perfect.

The twins were in the center of the family room, where their grandparents were removing their sweaters. This was it. Annie looked at Mason and grinned. Everyone was watching as if the process were fascinating. When the outerwear was off, the room got so quiet you could hear a pin drop. The message on the front of their little T-shirts sank in.

"'I'm the big brother. I'm the big sister.'" His mother's expression was priceless as she looked at Mason then Annie. "Another baby?"

"Surprise!" they said together.

The tiny guests of honor were momentarily forgotten as congratulations and hugs were offered all around. It didn't last long because Charlie fast-crawled over to the tree and started investigating the wrapped boxes and gift bags. His sister willingly joined in and they had Uncle Gabe's present nearly opened before intervention arrived.

Annie and Mason watched the happy chaos, their arms around each other's waists.

"Are you happy about the baby?" she asked. "It wasn't planned."

"I'm ecstatic. Thrilled. Proud. So lucky. It's the best gift I could have received." He kissed the top of her head.

"Me, too. I feel so blessed. A traditional family is everything I've ever wanted. And you made it possible. I love you so much."

"I love you more," he said. "It occurs to me that we were meant to find each other. In a perfect world we would have met, dated, fallen in love, had an engagement, married and then had children."

"Our story isn't that," she agreed. "But it's perfect for us."

* * * * *

Be sure to check out
Teresa Southwick's next book,
Maverick Holiday Magic,
part of the Montana Mavericks:
Six Brides for Six Brothers continuity
and available November 2019!

And for more great romances,
check out these other books by
Teresa Southwick:

An Unexpected Partnership
Just What the Cowboy Needed
His by Christmas
The New Guy in Town

Available now from
Harlequin Special Edition!

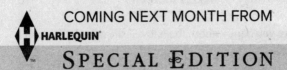

COMING NEXT MONTH FROM

HARLEQUIN®

SPECIAL EDITION

Available October 22, 2019

#2725 MAVERICK HOLIDAY MAGIC
Montana Mavericks: Six Brides for Six Brothers • by Teresa Southwick
Widowed rancher Hunter Crawford will do anything to make his daughter
happy—even if it means hiring a live-in nanny he thinks he doesn't need.
Merry Matthews quickly fills their house with cookies and Christmas spirit, leaving
Hunter to wonder if he might be able to keep this kind of magic forever...

#2726 A WYOMING CHRISTMAS TO REMEMBER
The Wyoming Multiples • by Melissa Senate
Stricken with temporary amnesia, Maddie Wolfe can't remember a single thing
about her life...or her husband, Sawyer. But even with electricity crackling
between them, it turns out their fairy tale was careening toward disaster. Will a
little Christmas spirit help Maddie find her memories—and the Wolfes find the
spark again?

#2727 THE SCROOGE OF LOON LAKE
Small-Town Sweethearts • by Carrie Nichols
Former navy lieutenant Desmond "Des" Gallagher has only bad memories of
Christmas from his childhood, so he hides away in the workshop of his barn
during the holidays. But Natalie Pierce is determined to get his help to save her
son's horse therapy program, and Des finds himself drawn to a woman he's not
sure he can love the way she needs.

#2728 THEIR UNEXPECTED CHRISTMAS GIFT
The Stone Gap Inn • by Shirley Jump
When a baby shows up in the kitchen of a bed-and-breakfast, chef Nick Jackson
helps the baby's aunt, Vivian Winthrop, create a makeshift family to give little
Ellie a perfect Christmas. But playing family together might get more serious than
either of them thought it could...

#2729 A DOWN-HOME SAVANNAH CHRISTMAS
The Savannah Sisters • by Nancy Robards Thompson
The odds of Ellie Clark falling for Daniel Quindlin are slim to none. First, she isn't
home to stay. And second, Daniel caused Ellie's fiancé to leave her at the altar.
Even if he had her best interests at heart, falling for her archnemesis just isn't
natural. Well, neither is a white Christmas in Savannah...

#2730 HOLIDAY BY CANDLELIGHT
Sutter Creek, Montana • by Laurel Greer
Avalanche survivor Dr. Caleb Matsuda is intent on living a risk-free life. But
planning a holiday party with free-spirited mountain rescuer Garnet James tempts
the handsome doctor to take a chance on love.

**YOU CAN FIND MORE INFORMATION ON UPCOMING HARLEQUIN® TITLES,
FREE EXCERPTS AND MORE AT WWW.HARLEQUIN.COM.**

HSECNM1019

SPECIAL EXCERPT FROM

H HARLEQUIN®

SPECIAL EDITION

*Stricken with temporary amnesia, Maddie Wolfe can't
remember a single thing about her life...or her husband,
Sawyer. But even with electricity crackling between
them, it turns out their fairy tale was careening toward
disaster. Will a little Christmas spirit help Maddie find
her memories—and the Wolfes find the spark again?*

Read on for a sneak preview of
A Wyoming Christmas to Remember
by Melissa Senate,
the next book in the Wyoming Multiples miniseries.

"Three weeks?" she repeated. "I might not remember
anything about myself for three weeks?"

Dr. Addison gave her a reassuring smile. "Could be
sooner. But we'll run some tests, and based on how well
you're doing now, I don't see any reason why you can't
be discharged later today."

Discharged where? Where did she live?

With your husband, she reminded herself.

She bolted upright again, her gaze moving to Sawyer,
who pocketed his phone and came back over, sitting
down and taking her hand in both of his. "Do I—do we—
have children?" she asked him. She couldn't forget her
own children. She couldn't.

"No," he said, glancing away for a moment. "Your
parents and Jenna will be here in fifteen minutes," he

said. "They're ecstatic you're awake. I let them know you might not remember them straightaway."

"Jenna?" she asked.

"Your twin sister. You're very close. To your parents, too. Your family is incredible—very warm and loving."

That was good.

She took a deep breath and looked at her hand in his. Her left hand. She wasn't wearing a wedding ring. He wore one, though—a gold band. So where was hers?

"Why aren't I wearing a wedding ring?" she asked.

His expression changed on a dime. He looked at her, then down at his feet. Dark brown cowboy boots.

Uh-oh, she thought. *He doesn't want to tell me. What is that about?*

Two orderlies came in just then, and Dr. Addison let Maddie know it was time for her CT scan, and that by the time she was done, her family would probably be here.

"I'll be waiting right here," Sawyer said, gently cupping his hand to her cheek.

As the orderlies wheeled her toward the door, she realized she missed Sawyer—looking at him, talking to him, her hand in his, his hand on her face. That had to be a good sign, right?

Even if she wasn't wearing her ring.

Don't miss
A Wyoming Christmas to Remember
by Melissa Senate,
available November 2019 wherever
Harlequin® Special Edition books and ebooks are sold.

www.Harlequin.com

Copyright © 2019 by Melissa Senate

HSEEXP1019

SPECIAL EXCERPT FROM

HQN™

*Seven years ago, Elizabeth Hamilton ran away from
her family. Now she's back to end things permanently,
only to discover how very much she wants to stay.
Can the hurt of the past seven years be healed over
the course of one Christmas season and bring the
Hamiltons the gift of a new beginning?*

Turn the page for a sneak peek at
New York Times *bestselling author RaeAnne Thayne's
heartwarming Haven Point story*
Coming Home for Christmas, *available now!*

This was it.

Luke Hamilton waited outside the big rambling Victorian
house in a little coastal town in Oregon, hands shoved into the
pockets of his coat against the wet slap of air and the nerves
churning through him.

Elizabeth was here. After all the years when he had been
certain she was dead—that she had wandered into the mountains
somewhere that cold day seven years earlier or she had somehow
walked into the deep, unforgiving waters of Lake Haven—he
was going to see her again.

Though he had been given months to wrap his head around
the idea that his wife wasn't dead, that she was indeed living
under another name in this town by the sea, it still didn't seem
real.

How was he supposed to feel in this moment? He had no idea.
He only knew he was filled with a crazy mix of anticipation, fear
and the low fury that had been simmering inside him for months,
since the moment FBI agent Elliot Bailey had produced a piece
of paper with a name and an address.

Luke still couldn't quite believe she was in there—the wife he
had not seen in seven years. The wife who had disappeared off

PHRTEXP1019R

the face of the earth, leaving plenty of people to speculate that he had somehow hurt her, even killed her.

For all those days and months and years, he had lived with the ghost of Elizabeth Sinclair and the love they had once shared.

He was never nervous, damn it. So why did his skin itch and his stomach seethe and his hands grip the cold metal of the porch railing as if his suddenly weak knees would give way and make him topple over if he let go?

A moment later, he sensed movement inside the foyer of the house. The woman he had spoken with when he had first pulled up to this address, the woman who had been hanging Christmas lights around the big charming home and who had looked at him with such suspicion and had not invited him to wait inside, opened the door. One hand was thrust into her coat pocket around a questionable-looking bulge.

She was either concealing a handgun or a Taser or pepper spray. Since he was not familiar with the woman, Luke couldn't begin to guess which. Her features had lost none of that alert wariness that told him she would do whatever necessary to protect Elizabeth.

He wanted to tell her he would never hurt his wife, but it was a refrain he had grown tired of repeating. Over the years, he had become inured to people's opinions on the matter. Let them think what the hell they wanted. He knew the truth.

"Where is she?" he demanded.

There was a long pause, like that tension-filled moment just before the gunfight in Old West movies. He wouldn't have been surprised if tumbleweeds suddenly blew down the street.

Then, from behind the first woman, another figure stepped out onto the porch, slim and blonde and…shockingly familiar.

He stared, stunned to his bones. It was her. Not Elizabeth. *Her.* He had seen this woman around his small Idaho town of Haven Point several times over the last few years, fleeting glimpses only out of the corner of his gaze at a baseball game or a school program.

The mystery woman.

Don't miss
Coming Home for Christmas *by RaeAnne Thayne,*
available wherever
HQN books and ebooks are sold!

Copyright © 2019 by RaeAnne Thayne

PHRTEXP1019R